The Office of
Historical Corrections

Danielle Evans is the author of the story collection *Before You Suffocate Your Own Fool Self*, winner of the PEN America PEN/Robert W. Bingham prize, the Hurston/ Wright Legacy Award, and the Paterson Prize, and a National Book Foundation '5 under 35' selection. Her stories have appeared in many magazines and anthologies, including *The Best American Short Stories*. She teaches in The Writing Seminars at Johns Hopkins University.

ALSO BY DANIELLE EVANS

Before You Suffocate Your Own Fool Self

The Office of Historical Corrections

A Novella and Stories

Danielle Evans

PICADOR

First published 2020 by Riverhead Books
An imprint of Penguin Random House LLC

First published in the United Kingdom 2020 by Picador

This edition first published 2021 by Picador
an imprint of Pan Macmillan
The Smithson, 6 Briset Street, London EC1M 5NR
EU representative: Macmillan Publishers Ireland
Limited, Mallard Lodge, Lansdowne Village, Dublin 4
Associated companies throughout the world
www.panmacmillan.com

HB ISBN 978-1-5290-5944-1
TPB ISBN 978-1-5290-6904-4

These stories have been previously published, in different form, in the
following publications: "Happily Ever After," for *Medium: Unruly Bodies*, edited
by Roxane Gay (2018); "Richard of York Gave Battle in Vain," *American Short Fiction*
(Fall 2016) and *Best American Short Stories 2017*; "Boys Go to Jupiter," *The Sewanee
Review* (Fall 2017) and *Best American Short Stories 2018*; "Alcatraz," *Callaloo* (Fall 2009);
"Why Won't Women Just Say What They Want," *Barrelhouse: Fall of Men* (Fall 2018);
"Anything Could Disappear" (as "Travel Tips for Young Women"),
Columbia: A Journal of Art and Literature (Fall 2012).

Lucille Clifton, 'i am accused of tending to the past' from *The Collected Poems of
Lucille Clifton*. Copyright © 1991 by Lucille Clifton. Used with the permission of
The Permissions Company, LLC, on behalf of BOA Editions, Ltd., boaeditions.org.

1 3 5 7 9 8 6 4 2

A CIP catalogue record for this book is available from the British Library.

Printed and bound by CPI Group (UK) Ltd, Croydon, CR0 4YY

Visit **www.picador.com** to read more about all our books
and to buy them. You will also find features, author interviews and
news of any author events, and you can sign up for e-newsletters
so that you're always first to hear about our new releases.

For Dawn Valore Martin

We know, in the case of the person, that whoever cannot tell himself the truth about his past is trapped in it, is immobilized in the prison of his undiscovered self. This is also true of nations. We know how a person, in such a paralysis, is unable to assess either his weaknesses or his strengths, and how frequently indeed he mistakes one for the other.

—James Baldwin

i am accused of tending to the past
as if i made it,
as if i sculpted it
with my own hands. i did not.
this past was waiting for me
when i came,

—Lucille Clifton

Contents

The Office of
Historical Corrections

Happily Ever After

When Lyssa was seven, her mother took her to see the movie where the mermaid wants legs, and when it ended Lyssa shook her head and squinted at the prince and said, *Why would she leave her family for that?* which for years contributed to the prevailing belief that she was sentimental or softhearted, when in fact she just knew a bad trade when she saw one. The whole ocean for one man. Not that she knew much about the ocean; Lyssa had been born in a landlocked state, and at thirty it seemed the closest she might get to the sea was her job working the gift shop in the lobby of the *Titanic*. It was not a metaphor: it was an actual replica of the *Titanic*, with a mini museum on the lower level, though most of their business came from weddings and children's birthday parties hosted on the upper decks.

The ship-shaped building was a creation of the late nineties, the pet project of an enterprising educational capitalist who wanted to build an attraction both rigorous in its attention to historical detail and visually stunning. To preserve history, he said to the public; to capitalize off of renewed interest in the disaster, he said to his investors. He had planned to build to scale, but that plan hadn't survived initial cost estimates. They'd only ever had a quarter of the passenger rooms the actual *Titanic* had, and most of those rooms were now unfurnished and used as storage closets, their custom bed frames sold secondhand during the last recession.

At the end of the summer season, a second-tier pop star rented the whole structure for a music video shoot, shutting down normal operations for three full days. Lyssa had been planning on having the time off, but when the video's director came to finalize the plans for the space, he'd stopped in front of the shop glass, stared for a minute, then walked in and said, "You—you're perfect."

She agreed to remain on-site for the filming and canceled the doctor's appointment she'd already rescheduled twice, giving herself in her head the lecture she imagined the doctor would have if he answered his own phone. Her coworker Mackenzie sulked around the ship for the rest of the afternoon, flinging herself into the director's line of vision without success. Mackenzie sometimes worked the gift shop counter with her, but only sometimes. Whenever there was a princess party, Mackenzie wore the costume dress and chaperoned as the princess-on-deck. Lyssa never worked parties; the one time anyone had bothered to give her an explanation for this (she hadn't asked), it was a supervisor who mumbled something about historical accuracy, meaning no Black princesses.

"We'd hate for the six-year-olds having tea parties on the *Titanic* to get the wrong idea about history," Lyssa said, so straight-faced that the supervisor failed to call her out for attitude.

"I guess they must want diversity," Mackenzie said after the director left, using air quotes for *diversity* even though it was the literal word she meant.

The next day, and, as Mackenzie went, genuinely conciliatory: "Maybe he wants to fuck you? He was cute, in a New York way. I bet he thinks you're exotic."

Exotic, not so much: the theme of the music video was sea monsters; everyone in it, including the pop star and Lyssa, would be painted with green body paint and spritzed with shimmer and filmed through a Vaseline lens that would add to the illusion that they were underwater. The pop star didn't want a ship; she wanted a shipwreck. Lyssa was just supposed to wear her regular uniform and work the counter and be herself in costume makeup.

Most of the real action took place on the upper decks.

In two days of shooting, Lyssa only saw the pop star from a distance, through the glass, but a longtime backup dancer gossiped about her during a coffee break. The pop star dedicated this video to an ex who told a tabloid she'd let herself go and looked like a monster in recent photos. The video was about letting herself go, appearing on screen green and fat and nearly naked. The pop star was thinner than Lyssa had ever been in her life. Lyssa understood why she'd been picked and not Mackenzie; they needed someone in the store who could look like she knew what she was doing behind the counter. She was backdrop.

But the director did, apparently, also want to fuck her, though it seemed as much an afterthought as anything, the kind of whim that came to the kind of man who always wanted to fuck somebody. When they weren't filming, the pop star and her assistant and her dancers traveled together like a swarm of fireflies, and the director and the tech crew and the hair and makeup artists were left to less glamorously fend for themselves. After they'd shut down for the second day, Lyssa's last day of filming, the director appeared as she was locking up the store and asked if she wanted a drink.

"OK," she said.

"I haven't been here long enough to find a good bar, but I've got a great bottle of Scotch back at the hotel," he said.

Lyssa saw the opening. She had been here all her life. She could tell him where a good bar was. She did not. In the hotel bathroom she scrubbed off the stubborn lingering bits of the green makeup and tried to look as respectable as a woman about to fuck a stranger could. When she came out, he had poured them drinks and didn't seem to notice she was fully human colored again. She took a sip and put the drink down and he reached for her hand, turned her palm over, and began to trace something in it.

"Are you trying to tell my fortune?" she asked.

"I wasn't," he said. "But I have a lucky guess that you're about to make a man very happy."

It was so gross it was almost endearing.

The first time, they used the condom in the hotel's romance kit, which consisted of a single condom and a package of after-dinner mints in a tin adorned with a rose sticker. The second time he pulled out, and the third time he didn't.

"Was that OK? I mean I know I'm safe," he said, a sentence that in her experience, men who were in any capacity actually safe never had to say out loud. "But are you on something?"

"You don't have to worry about that," she said. "I don't have ovaries."

"Hmm?"

"My mom died of cancer. So they took mine out. To be safe. See the scar?"

She turned onto her back and pointed to the faint line across her abdomen.

5

"I'm sorry," he said, placing a palm on her stomach.

"It's fine," she said.

"You don't have to pretend it's OK," he said.

"We don't have to be friends," she said.

SHE DID, IN FACT, have ovaries, but she also had a period you could set a watch by and an app that told her which weeks not to worry about carelessness. The scar on her belly was from an appendectomy she'd had as a teenager, and was the wrong direction for what it would have been if she'd had the other surgery. She was not supposed to still have the ovaries. A year and a half ago, her mother had gone to the hospital with what the intake doctor called textbook appendicitis symptoms and died of cancer eleven months later.

Because hospice was for people who intended to die, and Lyssa's mother didn't, she had refused to go. She died in the regular hospital, admitted through the ER, which meant even though she'd been remanded to the comfort care team, the doctor on rounds was officially required to come in once a day and report to Lyssa that her mother was still dying. He was kind about it, if not particularly attentive. Her mother was too drugged up to take the message herself, and the doctor was young and seemed embarrassed to be there, which was fair, Lyssa supposed—she too had stopped acting like this moment was anything but private. In the very beginning, when they'd still thought something could be done, Lyssa had gone to every new doctor's appointment dressed like it would be a photo shoot. She had bought clothes she couldn't afford, taken off early from work to press her hair, never met a new doctor without a full face of makeup.

There was always something they wouldn't tell everybody, and she wanted to be told, which meant she had to look like a real person to them, like a person whose mother deserved to live, like someone who loved somebody. Whatever information they weren't going to give her, whatever medicine they didn't bother trying on Black women, she would have to ask to get, would have to ask for directly so that it went in the file if they refused, but ask for without seeming stupid or aggressive or cold. She would have to be poised and polite through her frustration, which, thankfully, retail had prepared her for. *Tell me what you would tell a white woman*, her face said. *A white woman with money*, her clothes said. *Please*, her tone said. But eventually all the doctors told her the same thing, and Lyssa accepted there was nothing left to ask for. In the hospital at the end, she wore the same clothes for days and didn't bother combing her hair. A night janitor asked Lyssa if she was the patient's granddaughter; at first she was offended on her mother's behalf—illness hadn't aged her that much—but when she saw herself in the mirror, she realized it was not how old her mother looked, but how young she looked in her unmade state, how creaturely and unable to fend for herself. In the hospital bed, her mother looked alive and vital, only sleeping. *They often go as soon as you do*, a nurse said three days after they'd taken her mother off food, and Lyssa realized only much later that she had taken the wrong message, that the nurse hadn't meant Lyssa had to stay put or she might miss it. The same nurse pointed out on day five when her mother's urine bag had gone from yellow to brown, told her everything else would follow the kidneys and shut down soon.

Death would mean new logistics—administrators and insurance people. Lyssa showered in the hospital room bathroom, using the stinging antibacterial soap in the dispenser. She plugged in her blow-dryer and styled her hair. She put on a change of clothes, a muted-berry lipstick, and a sweep of mascara. When the doctor in charge of rounds came back, he looked at her as if seeing her for the first time. He asked her if anyone had talked to her about her own preventative options. No one had. He wrote on a prescription pad the name and number of the doctor he wanted her to call.

Lyssa thought she would talk to her mother about it, and then she remembered. She had to keep remembering, even after she'd seen the body and signed the paperwork and arranged a funeral. Somehow she'd expected the dying to be the worst part, that after it was over she could go home and tell some healthy living version of her mother about the terrible thing that had just happened to her. Lyssa felt cheated: out of a mother, out of a textbook diagnosis where they could have lifted the bad thing out of her mother and sent her home to recover. She was not ready to be cheated out of anything else. It took her months to call the doctor on the referral slip. She went to the appointment as her regular self, washed and neat, but otherwise unadorned.

"I don't have any children," she told the doctor.

"Were you planning on them?" he asked.

"I wasn't not planning on them."

The doctor sighed. He leaned forward and made a facial expression somewhere between a smile and a grimace, a face that looked like he'd practiced it in the mirror after being lectured about his bedside manner.

"Look, if you were going to try to have a baby tomorrow, I'd say perhaps that was your risk to take. But if you're not planning on starting a family anytime soon, well, you're not getting any younger, and I'd do this sooner rather than later. Take care of your real future, not your imaginary one."

Lyssa tried to imagine her real future. She had lived with her mother until her mother wasn't living. She had inherited the house, or whatever of the house she could get out from underneath the second mortgage, which locked her here for now if nothing else did. She could not imagine choosing the way her mother died, given a choice. But her mother had chosen it, had chosen, with her little bit of time left, every painful intervention, every last-chance effort, every surgical and injected and intravenous possibility of survival over comfort. When her mother asked and Lyssa said *this is not what I would do if it were me*, sometimes she meant *you are brave*, and sometimes she meant *you are reckless and foolish*, and sometimes she meant *I can't imagine what would be worth trying this hard to live for*. The first time she thought about dying, Lyssa was fourteen. She told her mother about the feeling and her mother said, "You'd have to shoot me first."

WHILE HER MOTHER WAS DYING, Lyssa was dating a bartender named Travis. She had been dating Travis before her mother got sick, though not for very long before. They met on Halloween, he liked to say, though it didn't really count as meeting in her mind—he had waved at her while she looked at him over the shoulder of a man in a pirate costume who was groping her and nibbling at her neck. Lyssa was trying to decide whether the pirate's gold tooth was part of the costume or part of his mouth when she looked up and saw Travis watching. Her costume had involved fishnets and a dress that wouldn't have made it out of her closet any other night, but she couldn't remember now what cheap last-minute addition had made it a costume— cat ears or vampire teeth or some kind of ominous hat. It was almost the end of slutty Halloween; last year, even the local college kids had been bundled into cartoon character onesies or dressed as clever puns, covered up like nuns, the real kind. But this was two Halloweens ago, and Lyssa hadn't known where things were headed, and wouldn't have known what else to wear even if she had. Mackenzie had insisted she come out, and then she and her friends had promptly disappeared into the bar's drunken throng, leaving Lyssa to her own devices. When Travis saw her with the pirate draped around her neck, her dress half off her shoulder and whatever costume accessory she'd been wearing long gone, he raised an eyebrow, more a question than a judgment, and when he waved, it felt like Lyssa was snapped back into herself and had the answer. She extricated herself. The pirate pled with her as far as the bar door, but when he realized that following her out would mean he'd have to wait in a line to get back in, he let her go.

She drove home to her mother, who had been waiting at the house all night with a bowl of candy that remained mostly uneaten. There used to be trick-or-treaters in their neighborhood, but since a few years back they had gotten only the few stray kids who didn't have a ride to the part of town with more expensive houses. Lyssa's mother insisted on overbuying anyway. The two of them sat at the table and split the leftover candy, sorted it into piles, sweet things from sweet-and-sour things, while Lyssa made fun of the party, the Halloween crowd, her own lackluster costume effort.

When she saw Travis again, back at his bar, it was almost a month later. She recognized his face but couldn't place it.

"How's your pirate?" he asked, and the night came back to her.

"Out to sea," she said.

Travis poured her a free beer. It was Thursday, and football season, so she had to compete for his attention with the television behind him. Lyssa had grown up without a team—her mother didn't believe in televised sports and there was no one else in the house to put them on, so Lyssa's one allegiance was to a college basketball team an ex had played for—but Travis's loyalties were evident from the jersey he wore. She adopted his team for the game, shouted at the screen at the appropriate times, marveled at the magic of sports: how easy it was to become invested, how picking one team over the other was enough to make things interesting, just a matter of making a choice. When Lyssa showed up for Travis's Super Bowl party a few months later, she was wearing a team shirt she'd ordered online toward the end of playoffs and had owned for only weeks, but both her fandom and their relationship felt true and legitimate, rich, even after their team lost, with the discovery that sometimes all it took to become something was to want it. The wanting felt like joy, but the joy was there because she'd assigned it to herself, and she didn't fully trust it. Certainly, the trick to everything couldn't be that cheap.

By the time her mother was first admitted to the hospital, the joy had started to feel like effort and Lyssa was working up the nerve to break things off, but Travis showed up in the lobby with flowers and a teddy bear, so it was too late then. Closer to the end, her mother ran out of the only painkiller that worked and Lyssa had to go to work. Travis offered to pick up the medicine and bring it by the house. Lyssa picked her mother's medicine up from the pharmacy all the time, and she never showed her mother's ID and rarely got asked for her own, but Travis was a man and a good three shades darker than she was. The pharmacist accused him of having a fake ID and asked him to come back with two other forms of ID and the patient. The patient was recovering from surgery. The patient could not get out of bed. The pharmacist said the patient's ID would not suffice. Travis argued, then he tried to call the doctor, then he cried. He was not a man who cried, but he had seen the condition he'd left her mother in.

The pharmacist called security and security asked him to leave. When he didn't, because Lyssa was still at work and her mother still needed the medicine, the two security guards pinned him to the ground, pressing him into the dirty red carpet and twisting his arm behind him hard enough that his shoulder was strained for days. It was only because just then the manager who knew who her mom was and had seen Travis with her before came back from her lunch break and asked what was going on that the cops didn't get called. Travis didn't tell Lyssa any of it happened. He said he'd hurt his shoulder lifting a keg. Lyssa only heard about it because the manager apologized to her the next time she went to fill a prescription. It had taken her a minute to even understand what she was being told, to gather that when the manager said, *I'm so sorry*, she didn't mean about everything Lyssa already knew was happening to her.

She called Travis from the parking lot and asked why he hadn't said anything. He said she had enough to deal with. Lyssa asked if he was OK, which felt stupid—it had been weeks already, and she knew for herself that his shoulder was better, had watched him, limber and shirtless, play in a pickup game just that weekend, though of course that wasn't exactly what she was asking, and anyway, he said he was fine. Later, when she told him what the doctor said, she half hoped he'd say, *Well, if it has to be tomorrow, we have a baby tomorrow*, but he just listened quietly and said, "If that's what you have to do to be healthy, that's what you have to do."

"That's sweet," her cousin said, when she tried to explain. "He wants you alive more than he wants you knocked up. Could be the other way around."

Lyssa was unsatisfied with these being her only options. She told Travis she was going to go through with it, then finally broke up with him. Lyssa went back to the doctor one more time to tell him no to the surgery for now, but she promised to come back and let them monitor her risk levels. So far, she had found a reason not to be at every scheduled follow-up and blood draw. Lyssa couldn't remember walking around without suspecting that something inside of her wanted her dead. What future had there ever been but the imaginary?

SHE WAS STILL not getting any younger. Maybe she wasn't getting much older either. In the dim hotel light, Lyssa noticed a green smudge she'd missed on her arm. The director was still talking to her, more interested than she was in being awake. She rubbed at the spot on her arm while he spooned her. She asked if it was true the pop star felt like a monster when she came up with the video concept.

"Who knows how she feels?" he said. "But she didn't come up with the concept."

"You did?"

"Her manager did. He's also the one who told the press her ex thought she looked like a monster. He thought she needed something to spark her. I was skeptical, but she was actually fucking magnificent today. It worked."

"For you," Lyssa said.

"We'll see." He breathed into her neck until he fell asleep.

In the morning, the director ordered them room service

breakfast and, after eating, went off to wrap things up at the shoot. Lyssa lounged around in the bathrobe and watched the hotel cable until it was late enough that she was worried the director might be back soon. The next day, work was closed for a deep cleaning, paid for by the pop star's people, though for months they kept finding glitter everywhere anyway. The children at birthday parties were mostly delighted, the wedding guests less so.

THE DAY THE POP STAR'S video launched there was a birthday party on the top deck, and Mackenzie was upstairs corralling a dozen tiny princesses. After declining for weeks, Lyssa had gone with Mackenzie and her friends to happy hour the night before, back to Travis's bar, where she had seen him with a new girl, felt a warmth for him as she'd watched him teach the girl how the bar's old pinball machine worked, steadying her hands at the flippers. Now she felt tender and hungover. Mackenzie laughed from upstairs. A wayward child—one of the princesses' brothers, wearing one of the paper captain hats they gave boys under six—wandered into the gift shop. He picked up a plastic replica of the replica and looked up at her with wide blue eyes. The hat tilted sideways on his head.

"Do you know this boat sank?" he asked.

"I do," Lyssa said. "Where are your parents?"

"If I'd been there, I would have fought that iceberg. I wish I could find that iceberg and kick its ass."

"Well, it turns out we've been fighting the ice for a long time now, and the ice is definitely losing," Lyssa said. "If you go back in time, you can tell the iceberg Antarctica is already melting and doesn't know it yet."

"Huh?" said the boy. Lyssa looked for something to give him, but the store didn't focus much on the disaster part of things—all they had in the way of iceberg merchandise were DVDs about the science of the crash and a plastic mold intended to make oversize iceberg-shaped ice cubes for cocktails. She handed him the free coloring page he had probably already been given at the party, and kept her eyes on him as he wandered out of the gift shop, watching until he was scooped into the arms of his bewildered-looking father, who carried him toward the stairs. Laughter rang out again from the top deck.

Lyssa slouched over the counter and looked up the pop star's video on her phone. It was a bad week for a breakthrough: Antarctica was, in fact, melting, perhaps irreversibly; a first-tier celebrity and her famous actor husband were having a messy breakup; the president had made a blustering threat against a country with an equally blustering leader; a kid with a gun held a fast-food restaurant hostage before killing himself, some of the video of the incident had been censored and some had not, and it was hard to know how much horror you were about to see before autoplay showed it. But the pop star was radiant, larger and greener on-screen than she had seemed when Lyssa saw her from a distance, joyful where in person she had looked morose. Lyssa was only on-screen for maybe ten seconds total. There was the underwater version of where she was standing; there she was lovely and monstrous, arranging the gift shop baubles, the snow globes and deck prisms pointing toward her, casting tiny shadows, leaving the smallest spaces on her body all lit up with danger.

Richard of York Gave
Battle in Vain

Two by two the animals boarded, and then all of the rest of them in the world died, but no one ever tells the story that way. Forty days and forty nights of being locked up helpless, knowing everything you'd ever known was drowning all around you, and at the end God shows up with a whimsical promise that he will not destroy the world again *with water*, which seems like a hell of a caveat.

Dori must find something reassuring in the story. Dori is a preschool teacher and a pastor's daughter, and she has found a way to carry the theme of the ark and the rainbow sign across the entire three days of her wedding, which began tonight with a welcome dinner and ends Sunday afternoon with brunch and a church service where, according to the program, her father will give a sermon titled

"God's Rainbow Sign for You." The bridesmaids' dresses
are rainbow, not individually multicolored, but ROY G.
BIV ordered, and each bridesmaid appears to have been
mandated to wear her assigned color all weekend; the red
bridesmaid, for example, wore a red T-shirt to the airport,
a red cocktail dress to dinner, and now red stilettos and
a red sash reading BRIDESMAID for the bachelorette party.
When assembled in a group, Dori's bridesmaids look like a
team of bridal Power Rangers.

Rena is not a bridesmaid but has been dragged along
for the festivities thanks to the aggressive hospitality of the
bridal party. She has worn black to avoid stepping on anyone's color-assigned toes, and Dori, of course, has worn
white. All night Rena has been waiting to judge Dori for
the look on her face when someone spots the two of them
and the rainbow bridal party and takes them for brides-
to-be, but so far they have only been to bars where the
bartenders greet everyone but Rena and the green bridesmaid, the other out-of-towner, by name.

There is a groom involved in this wedding, though Rena
believes his involvement must be loose; she can't imagine
JT is on board with this ark business. Rena has known JT
for five years. When they met, most of what they had in
common was that they were Americans, but far away from
home, that could be enough. JT was on his way back to the
States after a Peace Corps tour in Togo; she was on her way
back from Burkina Faso. The first leg of their flight home

was supposed to take them to Paris, but the plane had been diverted, and then returned to Ghana after the airline received a call claiming that an agent of biological warfare had been released on the plane. They landed to chaos; no one charged with telling them what happened next seemed sure of what information was credible or who had the authority to release it. The Ghanaian authorities had placed them under a quarantine that was strictly outlined but loosely enforced. Had the threat been legitimate, it would have gifted the planet to whatever came after humans. Instead, they'd been stuck on the grounded plane for the better part of a day, then shuttled off for a stressful week at a small hotel surrounded by armed guards, something, JT pointed out, a lot of tourists pay top dollar for.

As two of the three Americans on the flight, JT and Rena had found each other. The third American was a journalist of some renown, and so even after the immediate danger was contained, the story of their detention was covered out of proportion to its relevance. Reuters picked up none of the refugee camp photos Rena spent months arranging into a photo essay but did pick up a photo she'd taken of JT in his hotel room. His face was scruffy from several days without shaving and marked with an expression that was part fatigue, part cockiness, just a hint of his upper lip peeking from atop the loosely secured paper mask he'd been assigned to wear. It ran a few months later on the cover of the *Times Magazine*, with the text overlay reading IT'S A SMALL WORLD AFTER ALL: AMERICA IN THE AGE OF GLOBAL THREAT.

In that December's deluge of instant nostalgia, the photo made more than one best-of-the-year list. Rena had not lacked for freelance jobs since its publication. Aesthetically, it was not her best work, but JT, handsome, tanned, and blond, was what the public wanted as a symbol of America in the small and shrinking world, the boy-next-door on the other side of the world. Boy-next-door, Rena knew, always meant white boy next door. When America has one natural blond family left, its members will be trotted out to play every role that calls for someone all-American, to be interviewed in every time of crisis. They will be exhausted.

Rena was present in the photo, right at the edge, a shimmery and distorted sliver of herself in the mirror. Most people didn't notice her at all. One blogger who did misidentified her as hotel staff. In her line of work, it was sometimes helpful not to be immediately identified as an American, to be, in name and appearance, ethnically ambiguous, although her actual background—Black and Polish and Lebanese—was alchemy it had taken the country of her birth to make happen.

It was clear to Rena by the second day of their detention that nobody was dying. Dori phoned daily but stopped worrying about JT's physical well-being somewhere around day four, at which point she took a sharp interest in Rena. JT as himself had talked at length about life as an expat, mostly his life as an expat, but JT-as-Dori's-ventriloquist-dummy wanted to know about Rena's childhood, her future travel plans, her dating life. In some ways, Rena has Dori to thank for the fact that she and JT became close enough to sustain a friendship once the crisis was over. Rena guessed where the questions were coming from and wished that she had something to defuse the situation, to reassure Dori, but then and now, she had nothing. She had built the kind of life that belonged to her and her alone, one she could pick up and take with her as needed, and so there she was in JT's tiny hotel room, unattached and untethered and unbothered. To a girlfriend on a different continent, she might as well have been doing the dance of the seven red flags.

Dori is simple but she is not stupid, and since arriving in town for the wedding, Rena has wanted to level with her, but Dori will not give her the chance. Dori greeted her warmly and apologized extravagantly for JT's failure to ask her to take the wedding photos; Rena can't tell if Dori is being passive-aggressive or really doesn't know the difference between wedding photography and photojournalism. Dori has left aggressive-aggressive to the yellow bridesmaid, who materializes to interrupt every time Rena finds herself in private conversation with JT. Dori has negotiated her anxiety with perfect composure, but Dori has not womaned up and simply said to Rena, *Did you ever fuck my fiancé*, in which case Rena would have told her no.

What had actually happened was that Rena and JT

spent most of the hotel days playing a game called Worst Proverb, though they could never agree on the exact terms, and so neither of them ever won. JT believed the point of the game was to come up with the worst-case scenario for following proverbial advice. Over the course of the week, he offered a dozen different hypotheticals in which *you only regret the things you don't do* and *if at first you don't succeed, try, try again* came to a spectacularly bad end. Rena thought the point of the game was to identify the proverb that was the worst of all possible proverbs, and make a case for its failure. She'd run through a number of contenders before deciding on *In the land of the blind, the one-eyed man is king*. The land of the blind would be built for the blind; there would be no expectation among its citizens that the world should be other than what it was. In the land of the blind, the one-eyed man would adjust, or otherwise be deemed a lunatic or a heretic. The one-eyed man would spend his life learning to translate what experience was his alone, or else he would learn to shut up about it.

THE FOURTH BAR on the bachelorette party tour is dim and smells of ammonia. The bridal party sits around a wobbly wooden table playing bachelorette bingo, a hot-pink mutant hybrid of bingo and truth or dare—or, the bridal party minus the bridesmaid in blue sits. The blue bridesmaid is holding the bra she has unclasped and pulled from her tank top, and is striding across the bar to deposit it atop the table of a group of strangers at a booth against the far wall. She is two squares away from winning this round of bridal bingo, and this is one of the tasks between her and victory. The prize for winning bridal bingo is that the person with the fewest bingo squares x-ed out has to buy the winner's next drink. The winner never actually needs another drink. Rena has bought four winners drinks already tonight, but everyone is being polite about her lack of effort.

Dori is seated across from Rena and is, in infinitesimal increments, sliding her chair closer to the wall behind her, as if she can get close enough to merge with it and become some lovely, blushing painting looking over the spectacle. Dori claims to have been drinking champagne all night, which has required that she bring her own champagne bottle into several bars that don't serve anything but beer and well liquor, but for hours the champagne bottle has been stashed in her oversize purse, and Rena has seen her pouring ginger ale into a champagne flute. When Dori last ordered a round of drinks, Rena heard her at the bar, making sure some of the drinks were straight Coke or tonic water, for friends who were past their limits. Because Dori is the prettiest of all of her friends, Rena assumed she was the group's ringleader, but now she can see that this is not true. Dori is the caretaker. Dori turns to Rena, keeping one eye on her friend striding across the bar with the dangling lingerie.

"Sorry this is getting a little out of hand. I guess you've seen worse though. JT says you used to photograph strippers?"

Rena imagines Dori imagining her taking seedy headshots. Her photo series had hung for months in an LA museum, and one of the shots had been used as part of a campaign for sex workers' rights, but Rena isn't sure the clarification will be worth it.

"Kelly used to dance, you know," Dori says. "She was the first adult I ever saw naked."

"Kelly?"

"In the yellow. My cousin's best friend. She used to steal our drill team routines for the club. We used to watch her practice, and sometimes on slow nights she would sneak us in to drink for free."

"I didn't think you were much of a drinker."

"You haven't heard the rumors about pastors' daughters? Thankfully, I'm not much of anything I was at sixteen. Except with JT. I thought we'd be married practically out of high school."

"Why weren't you?"

"He went to college. Then he went to grad school. Then he went to Togo."

"Where were you?"

"Here," Dori says. "Always here."

———

There is a shrieking and then deep laughter from the other end of the bar. The blue bridesmaid, whose left breast is now dangerously close to escaping her tank top, has been joined by reinforcements, and they are dragging over a man from the table across the bar. He is muscled and burly, too big to be dragged against his will, but plays at putting up a fight before he falls to his knees in mock submission, then stands and walks toward their table, holding the bra above his head like a trophy belt. He tosses the bra on the table in front of Dori and tips his baseball cap.

"Ma'am," he says to Dori's wide eyes, "excuse my being forward, but I understand it's your bachelorette party, and your friends over here have obliged me to provide you with a dance."

For a moment Rena thinks this might be orchestrated, this man a real entertainer, Dori's friends better at conspiracy than she would have given them credit for, but then the man wobbles as he crouches over Dori, gyrating clumsily while trying to unbutton his own shirt, breathing too close to her face and seeming at any moment like he might lose balance and fall onto her. Dori looks to the bartender for salvation, some sort of regulatory intervention, but the bartender only grins and switches the music playing over the bar loudspeakers to something raunchy and heavy on bass. The bridesmaids begin laughing and pulling dollar bills from their purses. Before they close a circle around the table, Rena sees her chance. She is up and out the door before anyone can force her to stay.

*   *   *

It's a short dark walk back to the hotel, where the bar is closed and its lights are off, but someone is sitting at it anyway. Rena starts to walk past him on her way to the elevators but realizes it's one of the groomsmen. Michael from DC. He was on her connecting flight, one of those small regional shuttles sensitive to turbulence. He is tall and sinewy, and before she knew they were heading to the same place, she had watched him with a twinge of pity, folding himself into the too-small space of his plane seat a few rows ahead of hers.

"Early night?" Rena asks as she walks toward him.

"Let me tell you, you haven't lived until you've been to a bachelor party with a pastor present."

"Cake and punch in a church basement?"

"Scotch and cigars in a hotel penthouse. Still boring as all get-out. JT and I lived together in college, and he used to tell me he was from the most boring place in the country, but I didn't believe him until now."

"So you thought you'd liven Indiana up by sitting at an empty bar with a flask?"

"You never know when something interesting might happen."

"At least you got to change out of your rainbow color. Or were you guys not assigned colors?"

"We only have to wear them tomorrow."

"Men. Always getting off easy."

"Easy? Do you know how hard it is to find an orange vest?"

"Ooh, you're orange. Have you spent much time with your bridal counterpart?"

"Only met her briefly."

"See if you can get out of her what she did."

"What she did?"

"You have seven color choices; you don't put a redhead in orange unless you're angry at her. Girl is being punished for something. Must be some gossip."

"So far most of the gossip I've heard at this wedding has been about you."

"I only know one person here. Whatever you've heard isn't gossip; it's speculation."

"Fair enough," he says. "You want to finish this upstairs? Less to speculate about."

So now there will be something to gossip about. Maybe it will put Dori's mind at ease if Rena appears to be taken for the weekend. Michael tastes like gin and breath mints, and he is reaching for the button on her jeans before the door is closed. Rena affixes herself to his neck like she is trying to reach a vein; she is too old to be giving anyone a hickey, she knows, but she is determined right now to leave a mark, to become part of the temporary map of his body, to place herself briefly along his trajectory as something that can be physically noted, along with the smooth and likely professionally maintained ovals of his fingernails, the birthmark that looked almost like the shape of Iowa, the very slight paunch of his unclothed belly. She clasps a fist in his hair, which is thick and full, but they are at that age now, a few years older than the bride and groom, youth waving at them from the border to an unknown territory. Rena can tell that if she saw Michael again in two years, he would be starting to look like a middle-aged man, not unattractive or unpleasant looking, but it has snuck up on her, that time of her life when age-appropriate men remind her of her father, when you go a year without seeing a man and suddenly his hair is thinned in the middle, his beard graying, his body softer. So she is saying yes please to right now, to the pressure of his palm along her arm and his teeth on her earlobe, and she is surprised by how much she means it.

. . .

Sleeping in someone else's bed doesn't stop the nightmares. Rena observes this almost empirically—it has been a while since she has spent the night with anyone and a very long while since she slept soundly. It is her job to go to the places where the nightmares are. It is not a job a person takes if full nights of sleep are her priority. Plus, weddings are not easy. Rena has missed a lot of weddings by being strategically or unavoidably out of the country. The only time she was actually in a wedding, she was the maid of honor. It was her little sister Elizabeth's wedding, autumn in Ohio, a small ceremony, a marriage to a man both of them had grown up with, Connor from the house around the corner. Connor who used to mow their lawn and rake their leaves and shovel their snow. Rena's dress was gold. Her mother worried about the amount of cleavage and her grandmother said, *Her baby sister's getting married before her; let her flash whatever she needs to catch up.* For a week before the wedding, her sister had been terrified of rain, and Rena had lied about the weather report to comfort her, and the weather turned out to be beautiful, and her sister turned out to be beautiful, and Connor turned out to be the man who, a year later, suspected Elizabeth of cheating because he'd seen a repairman leave the house and she'd forgotten to tell him anyone was coming that day, and so he put a bullet through her head. She lived. Or someone lived: it was hard to match the person in the rehab facility with the person her sister had been.

Rena has not been to visit Elizabeth in three years. Her mother says Elizabeth is making small progress toward language. She can nod her head yes. She can recognize again the names of colors. Rena's sister was a middle-school drama

teacher, a job she had chosen because pursuing a theater career would have taken her too far away. When Elizabeth was
in college, Rena had come to see her in *Antigone* on opening
night, and though the show was not only in English but
staged, at the director's whim, to involve contemporary sets
and clothing and a backing soundtrack of Top 40 pop, Elizabeth told her afterward that she had memorized the play
both in English and in its original ancient Greek, which she
had taken classes in to better get a feel for drama.

There had been signs. Rena had been too far away to
see them, her parents maybe too close. Connor had threatened her before, but her sister did not say she was afraid of
Connor. The whole week of the wedding, her sister said
she was afraid of rain. All of her adult life people have
asked Rena why she goes to such dangerous places, and she
has always wanted to ask them where the safe place is. The
danger is in chemicals and airports and refugee camps and
war zones and regions known for sex tourism. The danger also sometimes took their trash out for them. The danger
came over for movie night and bought them a popcorn
maker for Christmas. The danger hugged her mother and
shook her father's hand.

THAT RENA WAKES UP screaming sometimes is something JT knows about her, the way she knows that he is an
insomniac and on bad nights can only sleep to Mingus.

There was a point at the hotel when they stopped sleeping in their own rooms and then when they stopped sleeping in their own beds, and even now she cannot say whether what they wanted was the comfort of another body in their respective restlessness or the excuse to cross a line, only that they never did cross it, and that tonight, before JT's wedding, she does not want to wake to a strange man holding her while she cries. It is 4:00 a.m. according to the hotel clock. She dresses in the bathroom and leaves, closing the door quietly behind her. Her room is one floor down and she is ready to pass the elevator and head for the staircase when she sees JT in the hallway. All weekend he has been put together—clean-shaven, with his hair gelled and slicked into place—but the JT she sees now looks more like the man she met, like he has just rolled out of bed. He seems as surprised by her as she is by him, and his face relaxes for a moment as he grins at her and raises an eyebrow.

"Where are you coming from?" he asks.

"Where are you going?" Rena asks. She is fully awake now and taking in the scene. It is four in the morning. There is a wedding today. The groom is standing at the elevator with a duffel bag. Something has gone wrong.

"I can't do this," he says.

Rena thinks of Dori, surely sound asleep by now, Dori with two years of wedding Pinterest boards, Dori almost certainly having rescued herself from the sweaty ministrations of the would-be stripper and then making her friends feel better about having upset her.

"You can't just leave," Rena says. "You have to tell her yourself."

"I'm going to call her," he says. "I'm going out of town for a little bit."

Rena moves herself between JT and the elevator to look him in the eyes. He does not seem or smell drunk, only sad. That he should be sad, that he should treat this decision as a thing that is happening to him, enrages her to the point that it surprises her. She speaks to him in a fierce whisper.

"When I met you we were trapped across the world, and you told me you were calm because you'd learned not to take for granted that anything was safe. You don't get to be scared of a woman you've been with since you were teenagers."

"I was scared," he says. "You were calm. You were so fucking calm it calmed me down, and that was what I liked about you."

"It's not my fault you're a coward," Rena says.

"You know," says JT, "I used to think you were so brave, and sometimes I still do, and sometimes I think it's just that there's nothing in your life but you, and you have no idea what it means to be scared that what you do might matter."

Rena flinches. She imagines slapping him, first imagines slapping the version of him inches from her face and then closes her eyes and imagines slapping the him from the photograph, slapping the useless mask right off of him. He wants this fight. People would come out of their rooms to see her shouting in the hallway, see a parting quarrel between old friends or old lovers or JT and a woman nursing an old wound. Excuses would be formulated; they would all calmly and quietly go back to sleep. JT is giving her a reason to give him a reason to stay. Rena does not stop him. She walks past him to the staircase and hears the elevator ding before the door closes behind her. The window in her room faces the parking lot, and she sees JT cross through the lot under the flush of the lights and disappear into his car. She sees the car flicker to life before he drives off, and she watches for quite some time, but he does not come back.

RENA FALLS ASLEEP WITH the curtains still open, and in the morning the sun through the windows is dusty and insistent as the banging at the door wakes her. Her body, groggy from sex and drinking, is temporarily uncooperative, but the noise continues until she is able to rally herself to open it for Dori and Kelly, the yellow bridesmaid.

"JT is gone," says Kelly. "He's not answering his phone."

Rena lets the other women in and pretends not to notice them scanning the room for any indication of her duplicity. She reminds herself that she is unhappy with JT and that this is not her fight.

"I ran into him in the hallway last night," Rena says. "I didn't think he would really go through with leaving."

"Did he say where he was going?" Dori asks.

"That seems like the wrong question."

"To you, maybe."

"Ohio," says Rena. The word has rounded its way out of her mouth before she has time to consider why she is saying it. But now that she has said it she keeps going. She invents an empty cabin belonging to one of JT's friends overseas, a conversation about JT's need to get his head together.

"OK," says Dori. "OK."

She sends Kelly downstairs to stall the guests and gives Rena fifteen minutes to get dressed.

THE ADDRESS RENA has given is a three-hour drive from where they are in Indiana, mostly highway. Dori buckles herself into the driver's seat, still, Rena notices belatedly, in her pre-wedding clothes—white leggings, a pale pink zip-up hoodie, and a white T-shirt bedazzled with the word BRIDE.

"I really am sorry," Rena says.

"You didn't tell him to leave, right?"

This is true, so Rena lets it sit. She is quiet until Billie Holiday's voice from the car radio becomes unbearable.

"What do you want?" Rena asks.

"From you?"

36

"From life."

"Right now I want to go find my fiancé before we lose the whole wedding day."

"Right."

At a traffic light, Rena's phone dings and Dori reaches for it with a speed that could be habit but Rena recognizes as distrust. The text, of course, is not from JT.

"Michael?" Dori says. "Michael, really?"

Rena grabs the phone back. Hey, says the text. You didn't have to take off last night.

Dori's relief at knowing where Rena spent the night is palpable. She turns to Rena with the closest approximation of a smile it seems possible for her to manage at the moment and asks, "So what was it like?" Rena understands her prying as a kind of apology. They are going to be friends now; they are going to seal it with intimate detail the way schoolgirls would seal a blood sisterhood with a needle and a solemn touch.

"It was fine," Rena says. "Kind of grabby and over pretty quick. We were both a little drunk."

"I had to teach JT. It took a few years."

"Years?"

"God, I did a lot of faking it."

"Maybe it wouldn't have taken as long if you hadn't faked it?"

"That, darling, is why you're single. If I hadn't faked it, he would have moved on to a girl who did."

"So she could have waited a decade for him to not marry her on their wedding day?"

They are at the turnoff for the highway, and Dori takes the right with such violent determination that Rena grips the door handle.

"My wedding day's not over yet. We could have JT back in time to marry me and get you and Michael to the open bar."

"There's an open bar?"

"We're religious. We're not cheap. Besides, my mother always says a wedding is not a success if it doesn't inspire another wedding. There's a bouquet with your name on it. Cut Michael off of the gin early and teach him what to do with his hands."

Dori is technically correct about the timeline; it is early, the sun still positioning itself to pin them in its full glow. In the flush of early morning light, Dori looks beatific, a magazine bride come to life. Rena has no idea in which direction JT actually took off, but it is possible that he has turned around, that he will turn around, that their paths will cross, the light hitting Dori in a way that reveals to him exactly how wrong he has been, and Dori will crown Rena this wedding's unlikely guardian angel. Until Toledo, there will still technically be time to get back to the hotel and pull this wedding off, but Rena saw JT's face last night, and if she knows anything by now, she knows the look of a man who is done with someone.

As for Michael, it doesn't really matter what she says about him; Dori is spinning the story that ends in happily ever after for everyone, the one where two years from now Rena and Michael are telling their meet-cute story at their own wedding. But Rena can see already everything wrong with that future. As a teenager, she prized her ability to see clearly the way things would end. She thought that if she saw things plainly enough, she could skip deception and disappointment, could love men not for their illusions but for their flaws and be loved for hers in return. She did not understand how to pretend. In her early twenties a series of men one by one held her to their chests and kissed the top of her head if they were gentlemen and palmed her ass if they were not and told her that she deserved better than they could give her. But what did it matter what she deserved, faced with the hilarity of one more person telling her glibly that better was out there when she was begging for mediocrity and couldn't have that?

Rena pressed herself against the emptiness, flirted with cliché: nights fucking strangers against alleyway walls, waking to bruises in places she didn't remember being grabbed. Though it had been almost a year of this by the time her sister was shot, her friends were happy to make retroactive excuses, to save themselves the trouble of an intervention that might only have been an intervention against a person being herself. So, more rough strangers, years she let make her mean. If she was not good enough for the thing other people had, who could be; if she did not deserve love, who should have it; if she could not find in a mirror what was so bad and unlovable in her, she would have to create it. She learned how to press the blade of her heart into the center of someone else's life, to palm a man's crotch under the table while smiling sweetly at his wife, to think, sometimes, concretely and deliberately, of her sister, punished for a thing she hadn't done, while raising an eyebrow in a bar and accepting a drink from a man who didn't bother hiding his ring. All the things she was getting away with! All the people who couldn't see beauty or danger when it was looking right at them, when it had adjusted itself and walked out of their upstairs bathroom after tucking their husband's penis back into his boxers, when it was under the hotel bedcovers while their boyfriend checked in on video chat. It was, if she is honest with herself, only because the circumstances were so strange that she didn't sleep with JT, that she didn't, one of those nights they woke up together, look him in the eyes and part her lips and trail her fingers down his bare chest and wait for what came next. It hadn't been knowing Dori existed that kept her from it.

Rena thought for years that the meanness in her would be hers forever, except first, the hard, mean thing about her started to sparkle; she began to advertise trouble in a way that made her the kind of woman friends did not leave alone with their boyfriends. Then the rage she'd spent a decade fucking to a point softened into a kind of compassion. Men seemed more fragile to her now, and because it was impossible to entirely hate something for being broken, she forgave even those men who'd left her teary eyed and begging for their damage. No wonder they had sent her off—who wants to be loved for the hole in their chest when there is a woman somewhere willing to lie and say she can fix it, another prepared to spend decades pretending it isn't there? She was, she wanted to tell everybody, so full of forgiveness lately, for herself and for everyone else. Her heart, these days, was a mewling kitten, apt to run off after anyone who would feed it, but try telling that to anyone who had known her the last decade, to anyone who had lived through all of her tiger years and wouldn't hold a palm out to her without wanting the chance to be destroyed. It was a lovely daydream Dori was having for her, but if Rena went to Michael's door speaking of her kitten heart, he would only hear kitten, he would only think pussy.

. . .

The awkward conversation fades into the comfort of nineties pop—God bless XM radio, the mercy of Dori changing the station before Billie broke open what was left of their hearts. Songs they have forgotten but now remember loving keep them company as they press through the landscape of rest stops and coffee shops and chain restaurants, slightly above the speed limit, so that things look even more alike than they might otherwise. By a little after ten they are at the edge of Indiana and Dori needs to pee, so they pull over at a rest stop off the turnpike. Rena follows her into the travel plaza to buy a bottled water and a packet of ibuprofen, her mouth still dry and her head faintly pulsing. The warm smell of grease activates her hangover, and by the time Dori exits the ladies' room, Rena is grabbing breakfast at the McDonald's counter.

There must be some law that any chain in an airport or rest stop is required to be just slightly off brand: Rena's hash browns taste congealed and suspiciously like grape soda, and her breakfast sandwich is dry and slightly oblong. Dori has a Coke and a sad parfait, which is so sad that she has downed the Coke before making it more than a few spoonfuls into breakfast. When she gets up to refill the soda, she walks by a man a few tables away, hunched over his own pitiful breakfast, the bottom of his gray beard dotted with a drip of coffee he doesn't seem to have noticed. His face breaks into a full smile as Dori walks by, and on her way back he calls, "Who's the lucky man?"

Dori freezes. For a moment her grip on the soda is so shaky it seems clear that she will drop it, that she will stain the offending BRIDE T-shirt beyond wearability, which will at least solve the problem of future commentary. But she keeps the soda in hand and composes herself as she turns back to the man with the beard, who has dabbed off the coffee with a napkin while waiting for her reply.

"All of Toledo," she says with a smile.

"Huh?"

"Bride's our band name. I'm the drummer. Show tonight."

"Yeah?" he says. His smile is still just as affable and natural; it is not the wedding that excited him but the chance to congratulate a stranger's happiness, and this endears him to Rena. She walks over to join the conversation Dori and the stranger have started regarding the imaginary band. He was in a band in college. The band was called Cold Supper. His name, fittingly, is Ernest.

"We never made it so far as the tour part," Ernest says. "Got out of the garage at least, played a few local shows. But never the road."

"Believe me, the glamour of the road life doesn't stop," says Rena, holding up the soggy second half of her sandwich.

Ernest smiles and pulls out a phone to show them a picture one of his old bandmates posted a few months earlier. A younger, skinny, and long-haired version of himself plays the guitar. He has not played in years, ten or fifteen, but he has a lucky pick in his wallet, which he shows them too. It is smooth to the touch and dips in where his thumb has pressed against it and has faded to the yellow of a smoker's teeth. Ernest insists on an autograph on the way out, promises to tell his niece in Toledo about their made-up show in a made-up bar, and so they provide him the autograph on a paper napkin, renaming themselves Glory and Tina. He waves them good luck on their way out. Rena flushes with shame. Ernest and his earnestness, his guitar pick, his poor niece in Toledo.

In the car Rena can't bring herself to close her door or click her seat belt, even as Dori starts the engine and the bells ding.

"I have to tell you something," she says. "I have no idea where JT went. I made the cabin thing up."

Dori is giddy with guilt and exhilaration from the life they made up inside. It takes a minute for her face to catch up with her feeling, for her eyes to go startled and her delicate features to scrunch together.

"You made it up?" she says. "What the hell address did you give me?"

"My sister's old house."

"Who lives there now?"

"Some people who sued their realtor because they didn't know when they bought the place that someone was shot there."

"Who was shot there?"

"My sister. By her husband. Two days before her first wedding anniversary. She's alive. She can't talk. Or maybe she can now. I don't visit."

"So this is your fucked-up cautionary tale? It's a good thing JT left me now because if he hadn't he would shoot me when he got sick of me?"

"I wasn't thinking that. I wasn't thinking anything, and I said the first thing that came to mind."

"The house where your sister got shot was the first thing that came to mind when I asked if you knew where my fiancé was?"

"It's always the first thing that comes to mind," Rena says, and she is too relieved by the honesty to be ashamed.

. . .

Dori pulls the car out of the rest stop lot and Rena prepares for the long silence on the way back. Dori will be too proud and polite to say what happened; she will only say they didn't find him. She will send guests home with tulle-wrapped almonds and be front and center at her father's sermon Sunday, by which point Rena will be on a plane home, home being a city she hasn't yet lived in, two weeks in a short-term sublet while she looks for a real rental, her belongings in a pod making their way across the ocean. But two exits later and many exits too early for that future, Dori gets off the highway. Rena isn't sure which set of signs they are following until they get there.

Waterworld. As advertised in highway billboards, except the billboards make it look giant and fluorescent, while in person it is somewhat sadder, a slide pool in one direction, a wave pool in another, and off to the side, vendors and a carnival stage with no show in progress. It is fifteen dollars to get in, but the real cash cow is the entryway gift shop, where now that they are here Rena supposes it would be rude not to buy a bathing suit. Dori buys a pink suit and a pair of blue Waterworld sweats. She is luminous. It is the first time all weekend Rena has seen her in real color.

"I'm sorry," Rena says, which she realizes only then that she didn't say earlier. Dori doesn't answer, and Rena follows her poolside, where they lock their phones in electric blue lockers with the paint scratched and peeling. KING SUM, someone has carved into theirs, and there is no explanation or response. On the other side of the lockers, there is a whole tangle of slides, the tallest of which has a long line, but it is the one Dori wants, and so they wait.

In order to go down the slide you must first go up, and halfway through their waiting they have come to an uncertain staircase, alarmingly slippery in places, spiraled and winding around a cylinder. The higher they go, the more Rena feels something like fear. Once she spent some time in Mexico, in the city where Edward James built unfinished or intentionally incomplete sculptures in the middle of a series of waterfalls: stairs leading nowhere, a lack of clarity about what was nature and what was built, a wildly unsafe tourist trap. This staircase should feel safer but does not, and by the time they reach the top Rena is giddy with relief at the thought of going back down. She seats herself at the start of the slide with something like genuine joy.

It is a fast ride to the pool below. At the third turn is a waterproof camera, the kind that projects the photo down to a booth where the operator will offer to print and frame it and sell it to you at an outrageous markup. Dori and Rena are riding together, two to a tube, down through a series of sharp turns, sprayed with water that seems to be coming from every direction, and then dropped into the pool, which stings first with impact and again with chlorine. Rena surfaces with an unexpected lightness, which she sees mirrored in Dori's smile. It occurs to her this might be the least terrible idea anyone involved in this alleged wedding has had in the last forty-eight hours.

Dori insists on checking out their picture after they towel off, so she heads for the photographer while Rena retrieves their phones.

Rena has three texts from Michael:

> Did I do something wrong last night?
>
> Did you kidnap the bride?!
>
> Hey, I don't know what's up, but get your perfect ass back here—there's an open bar waiting for us.

There are five texts from JT:

Where did you guys go?

Why did you think I was in Ohio?

Tell her I'm here.

Tell her I'm sorry.

Wedding is on! Where are you?

Wedding is on! JT has doubled back after all. He has come back to the place where whatever his decision is, it always stands. When Dori makes her way to the lockers, Rena hands her the phone. For a minute Dori's face is soft. She reaches for her own phone and reads through whatever amended case JT has made for himself there. She tugs on a strand of her wet hair. Then she turns to Rena and shrugs, turns the phone off, and shoves it back into the locker. She holds out to Rena the photo of the two of them. Dori's hair is whipping behind her, her smile open-mouthed and angled away. Rena is behind her, staring at the camera, laughing and startled. Dori has chosen a hideous purple-and-green airbrushed paper frame reading *Wish You Were Here.*

"This is going to be hilarious someday," Dori says. "I hope."

Rena stashes her phone in the locker with Dori's. There is still nothing at the carnival stage, and so they share cheese fries and cotton candy and make their way to the wave pool, where they rent inner tubes. Rena floats and thinks of the last time she did this, which must have been twenty years ago, must have been with her family when this was the kind of day trip they would have all found relaxing. When Rena would not have looked at the water and thought of E. coli, of hantavirus, of imminent drought, of a recent news story of a child who drowned in a pool like this because his parents sent him to the water park alone for free day care and no one there was watching for him. When it was still her job to keep Elizabeth's swimmies on, when there was still Elizabeth's laugh, when there were still seas to be crossed, when the whole world was in front of her. Wish you were here. Wish you were here. Wish you were here.

Boys Go to Jupiter

The bikini isn't even Claire's thing. Before this winter, if you had said Confederate flag, Claire would have thought of high school beach trips: rows and rows of tacky souvenir shops along the Ocean City Boardwalk, her best friend, Angela, muttering *They know they lost, right?* while Claire tried to remember which side of the Mason-Dixon line Maryland was on. The flag stuff is Jackson's, and she's mostly seeing Jackson to piss off Puppy. Puppy, Claire's almost stepmother, is legally named Poppy; Puppy is supposedly a childhood nickname stemming from a baby sister's mispronunciation, but Claire suspects that Puppy has made the whole thing up. Puppy deemed it wasteful to pay twice as much for a direct flight in order for Claire to avoid a layover, and her father listens to Puppy now, so for the first

half of her trip, Claire had to go in the wrong direction—
from Vermont to Florida via Detroit.

Jackson has a drawl and a pickup truck and, in spite of
his lack of farming experience, a farmer's tan. Claire meets
him at Burger Boy, the restaurant a few miles from her
father's house. Its chipping red-and-white tiles and musk
of grease give it all the glamour of a truck stop bathroom,
but it's a respite from the lemon-scented and pristine house
that brought her father to St. Petersburg for retirement. At
college, Claire mostly lives off of the salad bar, but here she
picks up a burger and fries to go every afternoon. It is the
kind of food Puppy says she can't eat since she turned
thirty, and Puppy, having no job and, from what Claire
gathers, limited ambitions beyond strolling the house in
expensive loungewear, is always home to miserably watch
her eat it. On her fourth Burger Boy visit, Claire picks up
Jackson too. They get high and make out in the pool house
that afternoon, and the next and the next and the next.

At nineteen, Jackson is six months older than Claire but
still a senior in high school. They try hanging out at his
house once, but Claire feels shamed by his mother's scru-
tiny, assumes she wants to know what's damaged or defec-
tive about Claire that has her screwing a high school boy.
After that, when they cannot be alone at her house because
her father is home (rarely) or Puppy is unbearable (frequently), they find places to park. He gives her the bikini
at the end of the first week, after she complains that her

father's move to Florida caught her off guard—she is used to winters that at least make an effort to be winter, but her father's new life in St. Pete is relentless sunshine, sunburn weather in December. Outside, by the pool, she has resigned herself to wearing T-shirts over one of Puppy's old suits, which is spangled with faded glitter and sags over Claire's bee-sting breasts. Jackson presents the bathing suit wadded up in a supermarket plastic bag, the sort of awkward non-gift you give someone in an awkward non-relationship—he bought it for five dollars on a spring break trip, he says, for a girlfriend he subsequently found blowing one of his friends in their shared motel room.

It isn't much—three triangles and some string—but the tag is still attached, and Jackson is beaming at her.

"You'd look so hot in this," he says.

She does look pretty hot: like someone she is not, what with the stars and bars marking her tits and crotch, but like a hot someone she is not.

"You look like white trash," Puppy says to her the first time she sees the bikini.

"You would know," Claire says back. The bathing suit becomes a habit, even after the temperature dips. Two days before she leaves town, she throws a pair of cutoffs and a T-shirt over it before she and Jackson leave the house, but when they get to the parking space—a clearing in a half-built, abandoned subdivision—she makes a show of stripping off the shorts and shirt. In the few minutes before he takes it off and fucks her in the truck's cab, Jackson snaps a picture of Claire, radiant and smiling and leaning against the crisp foil-flash of the bumper, the bikini's *X*s making her body a tic-tac-toe board.

She's already forgotten about the picture when Jackson posts it on Facebook that night, tagged with her name and #mygirl. Claire doesn't have the heart to object. On her last night in town she doesn't even see Jackson—her father takes her out for a fancy dinner along the waterfront, just her, and then it's goodbye. At the gate awaiting her connecting flight, Claire drapes herself over two airport chairs and checks the messages on her phone. She has eighteen new texts, most from casual acquaintances, the closest thing she has to friends at Dennis College. The messages range from hostile to bewildered, and it takes her a few minutes to decipher what has prompted them: a tweet from the account of the Black girl who lives across the hall from her, which features the photo of Claire in the bikini and the commentary "My hallmate just posted this picture of herself on vacation ☺."

Claire squints at the thumbnail photo of the tweet's author, the only Black girl on their dorm's floor, and vaguely remembers her. In the frenzied first weeks at Dennis, full of getting-to-know-you games and welcomes, Claire accepted the girl's friend request, but she wasn't really aware that hallmate was a thing, a relationship carrying some expectation of trust or camaraderie. She is strangely embarrassed by the picture, the way it turns her into someone else. She wasn't wearing the bikini to bother Black people—for Christ's sake, there were none in her father's new neighborhood to bother even if she wanted to—but to bother Puppy, who is half racist anyway, which makes her aggrieved reaction doubly hilarious. Claire turns her phone off again, closes her eyes, and thinks to the mental picture of the girl whose name she cannot remember, if she has ever known it, well fuck you too.

IN THEIR OLD Virginia neighborhood, in the old house, the one Claire's father sold the second she graduated, they have Black neighbors. The Halls move into Claire's subdivision the summer before she starts first grade, back when the neighborhood is still brand-new: tech money is paving western Fairfax on its way out to Reston, which will be malls and mini-mansions and glossy buildings soon. Claire's mother prefers the idea of a sprawling country house a little farther out, but her father likes the idea of something you can build from the ground up, tinkering with room sizes and flooring types, and so her father gets his house and Claire watches her mother choose from seven different shades of granite for the counters and eight different types of wood for the floors. Everything is so new and shiny when they move in that Claire is afraid of her own house, afraid her presence will somehow dent or tarnish it.

Though Claire has always lived in Virginia, and Virginia, she knows, is technically The South, Angela is the first person Claire remembers meeting whose voice lilts: the Halls moved from South Carolina, and the whole family talks with drowsy vowels and an occasional drag that gives some words—her name, for example—a comforting dip in the middle. In Mrs. Hall's mouth, Claire's name is a tunnel from which a person can emerge on the other side. Claire is fascinated by their accents, and, yes, by the dark tint of their skin, but mostly she is anxious to be seen. In her own house, Claire is alone: her only sibling is a half brother, Sean, ten years older, from her father's first marriage. She sees him for two weeks every summer and every other Christmas. Her father keeps long hours, and her mother has a certain formality; Claire loves her, but feels, in her presence, like a miniature adult, embarrassed by the silliness of her six-year-old desires.

Mrs. Hall is an elementary school teacher and has a high tolerance for the frenetic energy of children's games. Angela's house also has Aaron, her brother, who is only a year older than the two of them. Claire's mother refers to Angela and Aaron as Irish twins, which confuses Claire because they are neither twins nor Irish, so she adopts Mrs. Hall's term: stair-step siblings, one right behind the other. At that age, they are the same size, Angela tall for her age and Aaron short for his. Aaron is skinny and quiet and wears glasses that dwarf his face; Angela is a whirlwind.

Since Claire has no brother at home to torment, she and Angela torment Aaron together, chasing him around the front lawn, menacing him with handfuls of glitter and other arts and crafts detritus, taking his shoes from the row by the front door and hiding them in cupboards, in the garage, in the laundry. Claire, not yet entirely clear on the rules of family, thinks of herself as having not a half brother, but half-a-brother, and shortly after meeting the Halls she thinks of herself as having half of Angela's brother too. The first summer, Angela teaches her that silly hand game, which starts *My mother your mother live across the street*. Though this isn't technically true of them, it's close enough, so they swear it is about them, and torment Aaron with its refrain—*Girls are dandy just like candy, boys are rotten just like cotton, girls go to college to get more knowledge, boys go to Jupiter to get more stupider*. In most aspects Aaron is indifferent to their teasing, but the Jupiter taunt seems to bother him for its failures of logic. Boys, he insists, would have to be smart to go to Jupiter, and would probably go to college first. The argument has merits that Claire and Angela ignore in favor of papering the door of his room with pictures of Jupiter: crayon drawn, ripped out of magazines, snipped out of Claire's parents' dusty encyclopedia set, and once out of a children's book about the solar system, stolen from Angela's pediatrician's office. *How is the weather on Jupiter?* they ask him, though he never answers. Even now Claire recognizes renderings of the planet on sight, cloud spotted, big and bright and banded, unspectacular until you consider all it holds in orbit.

THE GIRL ACROSS THE HALL doesn't look like Angela at all. She is lighter skinned and heavier framed and her hair is wilder, deliberately unkempt in a way that would have made Angela's mother raise an eyebrow. Her name, Claire eventually remembers, is Carmen. By the time Claire arrives at her dorm room, on the second floor of a row of flat brick buildings that house a third of the small college's freshmen, there are forty-seven responses to and twenty-three retweets of Carmen's post. Claire is surprised by the level of interest, then annoyed by it. She distrusts collective anger; Claire's anger has always been her own. Claire prints a photo of the Confederate flag and scrawls in loopy cursive on the back WELCOME BACK! I HOPE YOU HAD A GREAT VACATION. When she slips the photo under Carmen's door, she means to tell Carmen-the-hallmate to fuck off.

The next morning, the voice mail on her phone is full. She has 354 new emails, most of them from strangers. Across the hall, campus movers are noisily carting Carmen off to a new dorm. A reporter from the student paper, unable to reach her by phone, has slipped a note under Claire's door asking for an interview. She gathers from his note that several bloggers have now picked up both the bikini photo and Carmen's photo of last night's postcard. She has a text from Jackson. The hashtag #badbikiniideas turns up 137 results, including one with a picture of swastikas Photoshopped into palm trees. An email marked URGENT informs her that her academic counselor would like to speak to her. In a separate urgent email, the Office of Diversity requests her presence. Someone using the email fuckyou fuckyoufuckyou@gmail.com thinks she is a cunt. Twenty-two different rednecks from around the country have sent her supportive pictures of their penises.

It seems clear to Claire that most of the hall has taken Carmen's side. Claire forgoes both showering and breakfast, opting instead to burrow in her room. Someone from the campus TV station has interviewed Carmen and put the clip online. In the video, Carmen stands in front of Bell Hall, one of the upperclassmen dorms, where she has apparently been relocated. She wears a Dennis College sweatshirt and wraps her arms around herself. "Up until this happened, I thought she was nice," Carmen says. "We always smiled at each other in the hallway. But she put a hate symbol where I sleep, and she thought it was funny." There is genuine fear in her eyes, which startles Claire.

Sean, who hasn't called her in months, has left an angry voice mail asking her what she was thinking. Claire does not call him back. Jackson texts again to tell her he knows she's busy, but he thinks she's awesome. Claire turns her phone off and shuts her in-box tab and spends the afternoon watching online videos of singing goats. She is on her tenth goat video when the president of the campus libertarians shows up at her door and introduces himself. His name is Robert and he lives two floors down, where he is the RA. He smiles like someone who has just won second place.

"I'm here in support of your right to free expression," he says.

"Don't take this personally," Claire says, "but unless you're here in support of my right to go to bed early, I don't care. I don't care about any of this. It was just a stupid picture."

"And you shouldn't be punished for it, but you will be if you don't get ahead of this. My friend lives on your hall and hasn't seen you all day, so we figured you were hiding out. We made you a care package."

The care package consists of a foil-wrapped caramel apple from the dining hall, which has declared it carnival week at the dessert buffet, and a book on libertarian philosophy, in case she's bored. Claire considers the offering. She is unimpressed, but also hungry, so she lets him in before his presence in her doorway becomes a spectacle.

"For the record," he says, "I'm not a big fan of the Confederate flag myself. The Confederacy was an all-around failure of military strategy. Lost the battle when they lost the ports, if you ask me. But I'm not going to judge anyone for their support of lost causes. As far as I'm concerned, you can wear anything you want."

Claire gathers that she is supposed to find this endearing, that she is supposed to bite the apple and lick the caramel off of her lips and ask him to tell her more about military strategy and let him plan her own response campaign, and that sometime several hours into this discussion she is supposed to end up naked out of awe or gratitude. Instead she sets the book and the apple on her desk, politely thanks him, tells him she is tired, and, when he finally leaves, locks the door behind him. She eats the apple alone in bed, figuring it can cover her meals for today and maybe tomorrow—she's still got some Burger Boy calories stored up.

When she checks her mail again before bed, there are another hundred emails. Her student account's address has been posted on several message boards and #clairewilliams vacationideas is a locally trending topic (Auschwitz, My Lai, Wounded Knee). She is losing on Twitter, but a group called Heritage Defenders has picked up the story and distributed it to their members, so at this point she has more supporters than detractors in her in-box. Cliff from Tennessee writes that when he was in college, his fraternity hosted an annual plantation ball for their sister sorority, and everyone dressed in their frilly historical finest. One year he and his frat brother decided to cover the house's front lawn in thousands of cotton balls, so that when they posed for pictures on its steps, the college's mostly Black janitorial staff could be seen in the background of the shot, cleaning up. PC police tried to shut down our chapter for it, but we stayed strong. "Hang in there!" the email concludes. There is an attachment: a picture of a boy, smiling wide in khaki pants with a button-down and vest, his arm around a laughing redhead in a corset and frilly hoop skirt, cotton balls blanketing the ground beneath them, a stooped Black man in a green uniform sweeping up cotton in the background. He has a broom and a plastic trash can on wheels and his uniform is crisp and synthetic-shiny—there's nothing historically authentic about his presence, other than his Blackness. She cannot see the man's face, but she can imagine it, and the imagining comes with a twinge of shame. But she is not Cliff, Claire reminds herself; Cliff thinking they are the same doesn't make them the same. The next email is angry and anonymous; its writer threatens to find out where she lives and set her on fire. Claire decides she will tell anyone looking where to find her. She prints out a copy of the flag and tapes it to her dorm window. She calls the reporter from the student paper back and tells him she is simply celebrating her heritage, like any number of groups on campus encourage students to do. She affects a lilt to say so, but as soon as the words are out of her mouth she realizes that the affect is a mistake. She doesn't sound like herself. She sounds like Angela.

————

IN THE SECOND GRADE, sometime after discovering that Angela is Black, Claire writes a poem about their friendship for Martin Luther King Day. Most of the lines she has forgotten over time, the exception being the dubious couplet "I judge her for her character / and so I'm never mad at her." Their teacher likes the poem so much that she stages it for the school's February assembly, assigning them costumes: Claire, a stiff black-and-white "patriot" uniform, complete with tricornered hat, and Angela, a kente cloth dress. For the next three years of elementary school they are dragged out to recite the poem every February, a performance that Angela's mother permits only after mandating a costume change.

Claire and Angela forever. By adolescence they have both lucked into beauty, but neither has really noticed yet; there is so little room for interlopers in the tight world of their friendship that they are often each other's only mirrors. When they are swarmed by boys at the mall, Angela will name the game, Wiccans or airheads or runaways, and they will play their roles until the boys catch on that they are being teased. The last good summer, they go to camp together at a college a few hours south of Fairfax. Other girls they know go to horse camp or dance camp or Paris, but they go to what Angela calls nerd camp. Technically they are not at camp together, because nerd camp is separated by discipline—Angela is there for poetry and Claire is there for language immersion—and most of the time all Claire can do is shout dirty words in French from across the quad when she sees Angela's group trooping to lunch like a line of maudlin ducks. But in the evenings everyone socializes together, and as the weeks accumulate, the counselors, who are only college age themselves, become lackadaisical about chaperoning and enforcing rules.

The third week of camp, a group escapes the confines of the awkward Saturday dance, flees the repurposed assembly room with its drooping crepe paper, the flailing girls on the dance floor ringed by a wall of scared boys who will not ask anyone to dance and are not cool enough to pretend not to want to. One of the photography campers has a water bottle full of vodka and someone else has a Tic Tac case full of pills, and at some point on their way to the most private patch of lawn they have taken pills and shots and then they are running through lawn sprinklers. Everything sizzles. When they kitten-pile into the grass, Claire turns to Angela. It is a love that requires touch, and so Claire snuggles against her, nuzzles into her neck to say it out loud against her. Love love love. Angela is her best friend, her other self. Someday they will go to college together. The world will unravel for them, fall at their feet.

A year later both of their mothers are sick. It starts slow, with both of them, and then quick quick quick. With Angela's mother it is a lump, with Claire's a vague malaise. We should have caught it sooner, Angela and Claire say to each other, over and over again, as though their mothers' bodies are their own. At first it seems as if, even in its cruelty, the universe is being kind, giving Claire a person to suffer through this with. Who else knows the smells of hospitals, the best way to sleep in a hospital chair, the flushed shame of disgust at cleaning up your mother's vomit, the palpitating anxiety of waking each morning thinking that this is the day something will go terribly wrong, the wince every time the phone rings while your mother is out of sight? Claire doesn't even have to give Angela words.

Aaron knows too. He is two grades ahead of them and supposed to be gone by now, but when his mother gets sick he defers his college acceptance. "Guess you were right," he says to Claire one afternoon, all of them in the basement watching daytime TV. "It's Jupiter for me after all." On-screen, two men on a court show are declared not the father, but one of them throws a chair at the other anyway.

"Jupiter would be better than this," says Claire.

One afternoon when their mothers are miserable and weary from chemo, Aaron finds Claire jogging in the rain, and pulls over for her. She cannot explain why, in spite of the storm, she hasn't turned around and gone back to the house—why she is, in fact, running in the wrong direction. When she gets into his car she sobs and then dry heaves and then follows Aaron into his house, where she strips and wraps herself in a throw blanket on the basement sofa and he makes her what his mother always made when they were kids, peppermint hot chocolate. It is out of season but still the best thing that has happened to her recently, though when she reaches for his body, feels the first thing she has felt in months that isn't slow death, that isn't bad either. He is still skinny, his hips slimmer than hers, so she slides underneath him; the weight of her, it seems, might smother him, but the weight of him tethers her to something. He is too gentle with her even after she tells him not to be; after he is finished she has to fake an orgasm to get him to stop insisting he'll make her come too. They don't love each other that way, or pretend to, so it isn't weird afterward, just a thing that happened because everyone is closer now. Claire and Angela can complete each other's thoughts. Claire and Aaron can be naked. Their mothers, who have only ever been casually friendly, now speak an intimate language of supplements and painkillers and hospitals and wig shops. Even their fathers have taken to neighborly gestures of solidarity.

Mrs. Hall has been Claire's second mother most of her life, and Claire fears that she will lose both her mother and her other mother, but it turns out that it is worse to lose only one, when it's the one that counts. Claire knows as soon as she feels it the first time that there is cruelty in this sentiment, so much cruelty that it surprises her, but that doesn't change the feeling. Mrs. Hall walks out of the hospital in full remission. Not a trace of the cancer left. Her hair grows back, soft and downy. She takes up running to drop the steroid weight. She is working up to marathons. Angela trains with her.

CLAIRE'S MOTHER DIES IN JULY. They bury her on a damp Tuesday when the ground is slimy from an afternoon thunderstorm. She does not hear a word the priest says, thinking of her mother down there, rotting. For weeks before the funeral she has nightmares in which she is the one being buried, alive, the sickening smell of earth always waking her. At the funeral, Angela holds her hand and Aaron puts an arm around her shoulders. He is a perfect gentleman, but one with a mother, and Angela is a friend with a mother, and already they are galaxies away from Claire, alone in her grief.

ROBERT IS NOT EASILY DISSUADED. He returns the next morning with a sandwich, a task list, and backup in the form of a short, freckled sophomore named Alan. By noon, Robert and Alan have sold Claire on their strategy. They tell her putting the flag up was brilliant, and that three other students have taped Confederate flags to their doors in solidarity. One of them, Robert confesses, is Alan. They have drafted a statement for her and agreed to a town hall meeting on her behalf.

"You're not breaking any rules," says Robert.

"You have a right to celebrate where you came from," Alan says. "Just stick to that and you'll be good. Don't let them make you sound like a racist. Don't let them turn you into your own worst enemy."

Claire's mother came from Connecticut. She found even the northernmost reaches of the South vaguely suspect. She missed New England seafood and would occasionally, when feeling extravagant, pay an exorbitant amount to express mail herself a live lobster. Claire's father was originally from Minnesota. Before he retired to Florida, Northern Virginia was the farthest south any relative of hers had ever lived. For the moment, it feels like a miracle to her that no one has to know any of that.

Claire has skipped her Monday and Tuesday classes, but the next morning is the occasion of her mandated appointment with the Dean of Student Affairs, the university ombudswoman, her adviser, and the Vice Dean of Diversity. She showers for the first time this week, blow-dries and teases her hair. She wears a horrible mint-green dress Puppy bought her for an engagement event that Claire refused to attend. She puts on her mother's pearls, takes them off, puts them on again.

It is a short walk to the ombudswoman's office, but by the time she gets there Claire is freezing, despite her coat, and wishes she had stopped for hot coffee in the student center. The office is wood paneled, newly renovated in a bright but bland way that invites you to imagine it decades later and dingy. Behind its windows, Claire knows, is the grace of woods in winter, but this morning the blinds are drawn. Claire's adviser, a twentysomething brunette whom Claire has met twice so far, gives her a tentative smile. At their first advising meeting, Claire noted that some of her student files were tagged with brightly colored sticky tabs. Claire's was tagged with red. The adviser was sheepish about it when Claire asked her what the color system was about, and Claire realized later that red must mean exactly what it looked like, though which disaster the adviser intended to mark, Claire still isn't sure. She doesn't trust a woman who puts literal red flags on things and expects people not to catch on. The ombudswoman is a middle-aged Puerto Rican woman in a drab pantsuit and the Dean of Student Affairs is a middle-aged white man wearing what Claire can only presume is one in an ongoing series of wacky ties, this one featuring cartoon insects. Together the two of them look like someone's embarrassing parents. The Vice Dean of Diversity, a thirtysomething Black man with dreadlocks and skinny jeans, has taken his own couch. He has his note-pad out and does not meet Claire's eye.

"We can't force you to take down the flag," says the om-budswoman, once Claire is seated. "I want to be clear that that's not what we're here to do. Your decor is not in viola-tion of any official university policy. But we can ask you, in the interest of the campus community and the well-being of your peers, to remove the flag from your window, and apologize to Miss Wilson. You will face a peer disciplinary hearing on the subject of your harassment of Miss Wilson, and I can only imagine that having made some attempt to rectify things will make a good impression on the disciplinary board."

"What harassment?"

"The threat you slipped under Miss Wilson's door," says the Vice Dean of Diversity.

"I threatened her to enjoy her vacation and feel welcomed back?"

"You left a Confederate flag postcard under her door," says the ombudswoman. "Aside from the fact that the image itself, sent to a Black student in the place where she lives, could be construed as a threat on its own, you knew already that Miss Wilson felt distressed by the image and was wary of your affinity for it. She reasonably construed it as a threat and requested that the university relocate her."

"A threat of what? That I was going to legally enslave her? Secede from the hallway, declare war on her, and then lose?"

"Please take this seriously," says her adviser.

"I only knew that she was distressed by the flag because she put a picture of me on the internet to harass me. When is her disciplinary hearing?"

"You, or your friend, put your picture on the internet," says her adviser, exasperation creeping into her voice. "We stress during orientation that nothing on the internet is private, and we wish more of you took that seriously. So far as we can tell, no one from campus had anything to do with publicizing your contact information."

"So a hundred people can send me death threats, but I can't put a flag in my window."

"No one can send you death threats," says the ombuds-woman. "If any of them are traced to this community, those students will be dealt with. And I would advise you to speak to both campus safety officers and the local police about any and all threats you receive. You're not on trial here. No one is out to get you, and none of us are on the disciplinary board. It is our job to ask you nicely to make this easier on everyone. What you do with that is up to you."

"The first thing I would do, if I were you, is take advan-tage of our excellent history department and talk to a pro-fessor about why the image you've chosen to go to bat for is so hostile," says the Vice Dean of Diversity.

Claire focuses on the window blinds and takes a breath.

"I am familiar with the Civil War and the student code of conduct," she says finally. "But bless your hearts for being so helpful."

Claire leaves for lunch feeling in control of the situation for the first time, and feeling in control of the situation is luxurious enough that she grabs lunch in the student cen-ter, not minding the stares. In an otherwise uneventful lit class, the professor seems confused by her accent, but Claire doesn't talk enough for anyone to be certain she didn't sound like that before. She heads back to her dorm giddy with relief.

When she first sees the photograph, it takes her a full minute to connect it to herself. One of the blogs that has taken to relentlessly covering the story and recommends she be expelled has posted a photo from the police file. There is her smashed-up car. There is a senior yearbook photo of Aaron. The article only has pieces of the story. Claire reads it to see if the Halls—any of them, all of them, Angela—have made any comment. The article says they cannot be reached.

IT IS NOVEMBER of senior year and Claire is hanging out with a girl named Seraphin, as in that is her actual given name, which never stops being hilarious. Or, Claire was hanging out with Seraphin, but who knows where Seraphin is now—her ex-boyfriend is back in town for Thanksgiving weekend and invited them to this party. Claire is three drinks? Four? Four drinks in to something bright pink that the host calls panty-dropper punch, one drink for every month her mother has been dead so far. She still thinks of it that way, as in, so far, her mother is still dead, but that could change any day now; any moment her mother could walk in and demand to know what she is doing, and what she has been doing, tonight, is drinking.

Grief has a palpable quality, and it is all she can feel unless she's making an active effort to feel something else. Tonight she is feeling drunk—pink and punchy and panty-dropping, because all of those things mean she is not at home, where Puppy has already strutted into the space her mother left behind with such velocity that it's clear to Claire that her father checked out well before her mother did.

Claire is still wearing panties, so far; she has that going for her, though she has held on to them only barely after an aborted tryst with a boy she met in the laundry room. She is barefoot, which she realizes only when something sharp startles her, which she has already forgotten by the time she gets to the other side of the kitchen and braces herself against the counter, but remembers again when she lifts her head and sees a streak of blood on the kitchen floor. *Shoes*, she is thinking, when she hears her name.

It shouldn't surprise her that Aaron is there. He has finally gone to college, but it is Thanksgiving, and there is so much to be thankful for in that house, so of course Aaron is back. He looks well. The freshman fifteen suit him. There is a girl on his arm Claire has never seen before— she is curly haired and caramel colored, and he whispers something into her ear that causes her to reluctantly leave them alone in the kitchen. So now Claire doesn't know two things, where her shoes are or who this Aaron is who has a life she knows nothing about. It has been months since she has spoken to either sibling. There is so much she wouldn't know about Aaron now, and yet standing in front of her he is a flip book of all the other Aarons she has known, from rotten rotten rotten Jupiter Jupiter Jupiter through last year in the basement, the grip of his palm on her hip.

"Claire?" he says. "You OK?"

"I'm fucking amazing," says Claire.

"You don't look good. Do you need me to call Angela?"

"For what? We don't talk."

"She's upset about that, you know. She has no idea why you won't talk to her."

"Because every time I see her I want to tell her I'm sorry your mother is alive, because it reminds me that mine is dead."

Aaron winces. He takes a nervous sip from his red cup before looking at her again.

"That's fucked up, Claire. My mom misses you too. You're messed up right now, I get that, but at some point you're going to have to stop making it worse."

"I'm not making it worse. I'm looking for my shoes."

"Where did you leave them?"

"Maybe with Brendan. He's in the laundry room. Probably still putting his pants on."

"Who's Brendan?"

"Who is anybody, anyway? Who are you?"

"Claire, enough. I'm taking you home, OK?"

There is something firm and brotherly in his tone and it infuriates her. She shakes her head, but he ignores her and comes close enough that he could touch her if he stretched out his arm. Claire lets out a scream that startles him into momentary retreat, a bestial noise she has been holding in for months. While Aaron is deciding what to do next, she is around him and out the door, the grass cold and wet on her feet. By the time he catches up with her, she is climbing into the driver's seat of her car. Claire leans her head against the steering wheel, suddenly exhausted. Aaron sighs from outside her open door. He hesitates for a minute, then hoists her over his shoulder and carries her around to the passenger side.

"Let's go home," he says.

She doesn't know whether he means her home or his home, but she is too tired to protest. Let him deliver her to her father's doorstep or the Halls' guest room, let someone who is still alive yell at her the way her mother is yelling in her head all the time. She presses her temple to the window and starts to fade out, only barely aware of Aaron digging through her purse for her keys and settling in behind the wheel, only barely hearing the yelling coming from some-where nearby.

The person yelling is Seraphin's current boyfriend, who is pissed that Seraphin went to her ex's party and invited him as an afterthought. Claire knows him, but not well. He's a little buzzed from pregaming but mostly he's angry, so when he sees, as he tells the police later, *a huge Black guy pulling Claire out of her car and rummaging through her purse*

75

and driving her away, he is alarmed enough that he and his friends get back in their car and follow Claire's, alarmed enough to call the cops while they're driving.

Claire sleeps through it at the time: Aaron, unnerved by the car behind him, flooring the accelerator; Seraphin's boyfriend tailgating, flashing his brights, then the car full of boys pulling alongside them, his friends throwing a soda bottle and yelling at Aaron to stop. Aaron only goes faster, losing them for a moment, then, less than a mile from their houses, turning onto Cleveland Street at such speed that he spins out and the car flips into the trees. Claire wakes up, vaguely, to sirens, and then for real, in the hospital, where she has a concussion and a hangover and a starring role in someone else's rescue story.

Aaron is dead. By the time Claire is awake enough to be aware of this, it has already been determined that he was not a stranger, that he was just above the legal limit, that people saw him chase her out of the party after she screamed, that she was passed out in her own car. The people who give him the benefit of the doubt mostly feel themselves to be magnanimous.

"He should have just pulled over and explained," Seraphin will say sadly a few weeks later, and Claire will nod, and Seraphin will be quoted saying it again in the paper when *The Post* runs an article about the accident's aftermath. Mrs. Hall will tell the reporter that a Black boy doesn't get out of the car at night in the woods for a car full of angry white boys in Virginia. Claire's father will read the paper and say it's not the 1950s.

It isn't; it's the first decade of the new millennium, but Claire's father is a lawyer, and Seraphin's boyfriend's father is Claire's father's golf partner. No one is assigned any legal responsibility for the accident. The Halls' lawsuit is dismissed before Claire has to say anything in public. It's Angela who won't talk to her now, and the tenth time Mrs. Hall knocks on their front door and no one answers, Claire's father gets a restraining order. Claire tells the reporter Aaron was a friend, that she was drunk and he was taking her home, but the bones of that story don't convince anyone it wasn't all, at best, a tragic misunderstanding; at worst, a danger she didn't see coming. Claire tells the reporter some innocuous nice thing about Seraphin's boyfriend, and the paper calls him one of her best friends, after which she stops trying to explain.

The Halls rent out their house for the spring and Angela finishes her senior year at a private school closer to DC. When Claire sees them rolling their suitcases out to the car, preparing to follow their moving van, she feels shame and relief, in which order she cannot say. Claire rides to prom in a limo with Seraphin and her boyfriend and a date whose name she forgets soon after. A month later the house Claire grew up in is on the market and her father and Puppy are formally engaged. Three months after that she is gone, tucked away at a small liberal arts college where no one has ever met her, and anything is possible.

Robert is at her dorm door again. She sees herself as he sees her, a problem to be solved. He is logic; she is x. The internet's discovery of the accident has driven the attention to a pitched furor. He wants to prepare her for the town hall that has been called regarding her continued presence on campus. Claire is not even sure she likes Robert, let alone trusts him, but she tells him everything. Someone has found a photograph of Aaron, the one that ran with his obituary. His smile melts into the part of Claire that still remembers when he was missing his two front teeth.

Aaron's favorite joke:

Knock-knock.
Who's there?
Anticipation.
Anticipation who?
. . .
Who?
. . .
. . .

It takes Claire and Angela more than a year to stop falling for it, to realize that the joke is their own impatience, not a punch line he's been holding out on them. Even as teenagers, they sometimes take the bait; they don't put it past him to have been waiting years for the right moment of revelation, for the payoff they've been promised.

THE TOWN HALL is held in the library's rotunda. The evening has been devised as an open mic, moderated by the Vice Dean of Diversity and the Dean of Students. People who do not wish to speak may make comments on note cards and drop them in boxes at the end of each row. The cards will be periodically collected and read aloud. Robert has provided Claire with an annotated list of episodes of Confederate valor or sacrifice, anything she might say she believes the flag stands for. She scans it for highlights: Albert Johnson, who sent his personal doctors to treat injured Union soldiers while he bled out on the battlefield—don't mention that he probably didn't know he was shot—the point is a crueler man might have lived. Thirty-two hundred African American Confederate veterans. Such a young army; so many dead boys.

Claire is wearing a dress marked with yellow flowers. The first person to speak is a weepy white sophomore boy, who expresses how distraught he is to be on a campus that has been touched by hate and personally apologizes to the Black students on campus, which apology takes the full remaining three minutes of his allotted time. Claire watches Carmen, who does not look in her direction. Carmen is surrounded by two full rows of Black students, more Black people than Claire has ever seen on campus before—maybe, it occurs to her, more Black people than Claire has ever seen at once in her life. None of them stand to speak. A boy in a vest and fedora approaches the microphone and dramatically reads the lyrics of "Sweet Home Alabama." No one can determine whether or not he is being ironic.

Robert has told Claire to wait for as close to the end as possible, to let everyone rage against her and then win with the last word. Claire waits.

She is only supposed to talk about Aaron if somebody asks. She is supposed to say accident as many times as she possibly can. She is supposed to say that he was one of her best friends and she is insulted by any speculation to the contrary. She has practiced saying these things as truths and saying them as lies. I killed someone. I loved him. I walked away. A warped version of that icebreaker game. Two truths and a lie, or two lies and a truth.

After the boy in the fedora finishes, two other white students speak, and then the microphone stands unattended. None of the Black students move. At first Claire thinks their silence is hesitation, but everyone remains still long beyond awkwardness—ten minutes, exactly. One by one the Black students stand. They hand their note cards to the Dean of Students, and then they leave. The Dean turns over card after card after card; all of them are blank. Handfuls of white students begin to stand, gather their things, and file out behind them. Robert is scribbling a note.

Claire has come prepared for an argument. She does not know how to resist this enveloping silence. It is strategic. It hums in her head. But the room is still half full. The microphone is still on. There are three reporters from the student paper, and ten from national news outlets. There are still ten feet between her and the echoing sound of her own voice, telling her she can still be anybody she wants to.

Alcatraz

Everyone had told me that Alcatraz was nothing but a tourist trap, but I was desperate that summer for anything that would give my mother a sense of closure, and it seemed fortuitous that the prison that had opened all the wounds in the first place was right in the middle of the water I could see from the window of my new apartment. I hadn't come to the Bay on purpose—a string of coincidences and a life I hadn't known I'd wanted until I got there brought me to Oakland. Still, almost since the day I had arrived, it seemed like the only thing keeping me from the island was deliberate avoidance. I felt like I'd gotten it backward. Everyone else I'd met who'd come to California from the East Coast was running away from something, and

I'd gone and gotten so close to the sting of the past that it sometimes seemed like I could touch it.

I had come west to work at an experimental after-school theater and dance therapy program for children who had been abused. A friend I'd gone to college with spent months recruiting me, sending me literature about the program: smiling children's faces, photographs of the Bay and the Pacific. I was sold on the adventure, on the postcard-perfect water's specific shade of blue, but by the time I said yes, she'd decided to move to Texas to begin a PhD program. I went anyway—I was twenty-four and convinced that the life in which I made some critically important difference to everyone around me could start on my command, that the world was only waiting to know what I asked of it. I was anxious and exhausted all the time then, but I remember those days now as being filled with optimism, a sense of possibility.

The organization's budget was so strained that our supervisors worked for free some months when we were between grants. I made ends meet tutoring and doing SAT prep for kids in Berkeley and Marin County. Two of our college student volunteers quit after working at the center for less than a week—one of them had her cell phone stolen and the other was cursed out by four different kids, in three different languages. My own first week on the job, a child had threatened to stab me with a pencil, but by and large I loved the work I did, the crayon drawings and ear-

nest thank-you letters I got to pin to my wall, the way kids
who used to greet me with skittishness at best, open con-
tempt and hostility at worst, started running to hug me when
I walked through the door.

MY MOTHER had never been to the West Coast and didn't
like that I was there. We were East Coast people and this
coast had done us wrong, almost kept us from existing. My
great-grandfather had done time here—had been kept in
the basement of Alcatraz, and been told every day that when
he was dead they would feed him to the rats. He was eighteen then, finally of legal age to be in the army, except he'd
been in it three years already thanks to a falsified birth certificate. It was 1920 and Alcatraz was still a military prison,
infamous not for its gangsters but among would-be desert-
ers. They were still building the parts of the prison that
would later be immortalized, but it was already enough of a
prison to be Charles Sullivan's private hell, the one he never
really left, the one my mother, God bless her, was still trying
to redeem.

My mother was born nearly four decades later, born at
all because after two years, the army, with the help of his
appointed lawyer, admitted their mistake. They cleared him
of murder and told him he was free to go. He took the long
way back to the Bronx—spent years trying to make himself
homes in inhospitable places—but when he finally arrived

back in New York, he married Louise, the first woman who took pity on him, and they had two children, the younger of whom was my grandmother. I never met her; she left a few months after my mother—a brown girl in a white family—was born. When my mother was six, a neighbor told her to her face that her own mother was too ashamed to stay in the house and claim her. After she came home crying, Charlie Sullivan pricked his finger and then hers and pressed them together and said they had the same blood now and whatever she was he was too, but my mother was too young to have heard of the one-drop rule and the intention was lost on her until years later. My mother called her grandparents Grammy and Papa: Grammy was firmly assigned the role of grandparent because they all chose to believe her mother might return someday, but Papa was her everything. When she was thirteen, her Grammy died, and my mother belatedly came to appreciate what she had done while alive—squirreled away money before Papa spent it, saw to it that the rent was paid and the heat was on and everyone in the house had clean clothes and three meals a day, and that her husband stayed sober enough to work, except when he had the prison nightmares, and had to be kept drunk enough not to wake the neighbors with screams.

At eighteen, my mother left home for college. She only went as far as Jersey, but her grandfather was dead within two years of her going. It wouldn't occur to me until well into my adulthood, most of it spent in California, a full country away from her, to question my mother's conviction that the former event had caused the latter, or to wonder what she wanted me to do with a cautionary tale in which the caution was against growing up.

BY THE TIME SHE CAME to visit me in Oakland, my mother had been involved in some form of litigation or negotiation with the U.S. government for the better part of twenty years. Her latest calculations—which she had me double-check annually, adding the accrued interest— concluded that the U.S. government owed us $227,035.87. She wanted the number exact so that we did not seem un- reasonable. I was a kid when she started the complaint pro- cess, first with letters to the Board for Correction of Military records, the same board her grandfather had been writing letters to for years before he died. This was right after my parents' divorce, though I'm not sure it's fair to imply the correlation. Before the divorce they had fights about the fact that she wouldn't sell any of Papa's old belongings, or dispose of the boxes of paperwork, but it wasn't those fights or any other that finally broke them up so much as the way they had less and less to say to one another when they were happy. With my father out of the house, my mother threw herself into a mission to clear her grandfather's name, to finish in her lifetime what he hadn't been able to finish in his. There were no adults around to talk her out of it, only me. She asked me what I would do if someone told a lie about her, asked if she died with it still written down somewhere, whether I would ever give up fighting to prove the truth. I knew that the only correct answer was no.

Her odds of succeeding were low. When she started the process, it had been fifteen years since Papa's death, and more than seventy since the conviction. Still, there was a logic to her argument—the discharge paperwork she kept carbon copies of in our attic said he'd been pardoned, and she thought it would be easy, from there, to have his dishonorable discharge changed to an honorable one. It didn't make sense, she reasoned, that if he'd been cleared of the crime he was accused of, that the government should consider him dishonorable. As years passed without action or response, she was buoyed by occasional signs of what she saw as precedent on her side. In 1999, Lt. Henry Flipper, the first Black graduate of West Point, had been given a posthumous presidential pardon, more than a hundred years after he was falsely charged with embezzlement in a scandal designed to push him out of the service. My mother had bought a bottle of champagne and shared it with me while we watched the official pardon ceremony, where descendants of the late Lt. Flipper sat on a podium with Bill Clinton and Colin Powell and received a formal apology.

"Do you see what happens," my mother had asked me, "when you don't give up on making things right?"

But what I'd seen happen—before that brief moment of optimism and especially in the five years since—was my mother becoming increasingly dependent on an outcome that seemed less and less likely. She taught elementary school, but all of her holiday breaks, half days, and weekends went into the litigation, into letters to the army, the president, her congressman. Not counting our hourly labor, my mother must have already spent almost half of the $220,000 we were theoretically owed on court filing fees, photocopies, and certified letters. When I had lived at home, my spare time went into organizing the files, photocopying important documents, holding my breath. Two months after I moved to Oakland, the Supreme Court denied my mother's request that they hear her appeal against the VA. My mother called from the other side of the country, sounding defeated. There was nobody left to argue with.

"Papa will never have his name back," she said.

"You know who he was," I said, but it didn't seem to comfort her any.

After I got off the phone with her, I'd felt helpless, and finally booked a reservation on one of the Alcatraz tour boats. When I got out to the docks at my appointed time, I couldn't bring myself to actually get on the boat. I'd milled around Fisherman's Wharf instead, ducking out of tourists' snapshots and trying to name the source of my unease. I'd watched the water for a while—the same fierce, unwavering blue of it that I felt had called me here—and ended up stopping at one of the gift shops on the pier and buying my mother a poster commemorating the Native American takeover of the island. Alcatraz Indians, it said on the front, under a cartoonish picture of something half man, half eagle. *I thought it might be easier to remember that this could also be a place of freedom*, I scrawled on the back. She never mentioned receiving it.

Reticence was not my mother's nature, and when, in the weeks that followed, she had less and less to say about anything, I panicked. She was still a few weeks away from the start of the school year. I insisted she come out to visit me. I wanted to see for myself how bad things were with her.

She arrived twenty pounds lighter than when I'd seen her a few months ago. My mother, who lived in discount denim and told me once that she found mascara unseemly, was wearing makeup and designer heels. If I hadn't known she didn't believe in mood-altering drugs, I would have taken her for heavily medicated. She was dressed like an actress auditioning for the part of my mother in a movie. A different daughter might have been reassured, but I looked at my mother and saw a person directing all of her energy toward being outwardly composed because the inside was a lost cause.

"How are you doing?" I asked her once we'd gotten back from the airport and settled her into my apartment.

"How do you think?" she asked.

I offered to sleep on the couch and give her the bed-room, but she refused, and most nights passed out on the couch by ten, after watching syndicated sitcoms and having two glasses of wine. When I'd imagined her having more time for normalcy when the case was over, I hadn't imagined this. Nothing I suggested excited or distracted her. When pressed, she made increasingly bizarre plans for the future. She was moving in with me, never mind that she had a house full of things on the other side of the country. She was moving to France, never mind that she didn't speak French. She was joining the Peace Corps, never mind that she was in her late forties and had never so much as been camping because she didn't understand why anyone would voluntarily separate themselves from reliable indoor plumbing.

It was probably my mother's focus on unlikely and un-reasonable futures that gave me the idea that I could still fix something for her. I found Nancy Morton, who was techni-cally my mother's first cousin, and, besides me, her last liv-ing relative. Nancy was Charlie Sullivan's granddaughter too, and my mother had not seen her since his funeral. The fam-ily's failure to bridge their divide in her generation was on her list of ways Papa's legacy was being dishonored.

I'd already made arrangements with Nancy and booked the boat tickets by the time I explained the plan to my mother. She was wary. She had tried to reach out to her cousins when the litigation first began and her letter had come back marked return to sender from the address she had for Nancy's older brother.

"They're still your family," I insisted.

"They are *not* my family," my mother said. "We're just related."

I'd finally convinced her that the whole trip was what her grandfather would have wanted for us, because I had her own words on my side. Almost immediately, I had doubts about the brilliance of my plan, but it was too late. I'd invited a group of practical strangers to meet us on a boat, and now here we were—instant family, just add water.

. . .

It was uncharacteristically hot for the Bay Area in August. The air felt thick and stifling like the East Coast summers I had left behind. Nancy Morton kept pulling an economy-size bottle of sunscreen out of her giant straw handbag and slathering gobs of it on her already reddening skin. Her husband, Ken, kept staring at his sneakers. He had barely spoken since we'd all done handshakes and introductions at the pier. Actually, he had spoken exactly six words since then, those words being "Kelli, put your damn clothes on," when their younger daughter had taken off her damp T-shirt and begun walking around in her bikini top. Their older daughter, Sarah, was twenty-three—we shared a birthday, though a year apart—and looked as embarrassed by her family as I was.

This was only the third time that my mother and Nancy had seen each other. When they were small children, Nancy and her brother had been brought to their grandparents' house for monthly visits, on the condition that my mother was out of the house. By six, my mother understood that she was Black and her family was not, and this was why the rule existed, but her understanding was impersonal and matter-of-fact; it was a rule like gravity, one from a higher authority. From the window of the neighbor's apartment where she'd been sent, my mother could see Nancy on the front steps of their grandparents' building. She was a small girl with a long blond braid hanging down her back; it brushed against the dingy ground as Nancy did her best to flatten a series of bottle caps with a rock. My mother was generally obedient, but her curiosity and her nagging sense that other children weren't sent away when their families came by got the best of her; while the neighbor who was supposed to be keeping an eye on her watched her stories in the bedroom, my mother went downstairs and peeked through the glass of the front door to get a better look at Nancy, who finally looked up and pressed her face against the other side of the glass to look back. My mother opened the door.

"Why were you watching me?" Nancy asked.

"We're cousins," said my mother. "And your hair looks pretend."

"Is not," said Nancy. "And I don't have cousins."

"Do too. I live here. With our Grammy and Papa."

The names meant nothing to Nancy, who called them
Grandpa and Grandma Sullivan, but my mother offered as
evidence the locket around her neck, the one with her
grandparents' pictures sealed in it. It was convincing enough
for Nancy, who shrieked and hugged her. Nancy offered her
a flattened bottle cap, and when my mother said it looked
like a coin, they got the idea to play store, make-believe buying and selling flowers and dirt from the backyard and the
clothing and jewelry they were wearing. They were absorbed
enough not to notice that Nancy's parents had emerged from
the apartment and were on their way out until after Nancy's
mother opened the front door and saw them playing together.

She screamed her daughter's name and grabbed Nancy
by her pigtail, pulling her by her hair down the block to
their car, Nancy's neck straining unnaturally backward the
whole way. My mother, afraid Nancy's mother would come
back for it, clutched the bottle cap in her hand so tightly
that it sliced her skin. Nancy cried hysterically as her mother
shoved her into the back seat and slammed the door, without a word to or from her husband, who took his son's
hand, followed his wife and screaming daughter to the car,
and started the engine without so much as saying goodbye.
My mother watched them drive away like that, her own
palm still bleeding. Nancy's tear-streaked face was pressed
against the rear window. It was the last time her uncle
brought his family over, the last time my mother saw him

aside from his parents' funerals. For years she told and re-told Papa the story of the game, as if she could find the detail that had made it go wrong, until she was old enough to understand that she was the detail, the wrong thing. *Someday*, Papa told her, *all this foolishness will be done, and all my grandchildren and their children will celebrate together.* But whatever it would take to make someday happen, it did not seem to be happening in her house.

"You have no idea how much you take for granted," my mother told me the first time I'd brought a white friend home to play. But she was wrong about that—you take noth-ing for granted when the price of it is etched across the face of the person you love the most, when you are born into a series of loans and know you will never be up to the cost of the debt.

. . .

"Cecilia is studying to be a doctor," my mother told the Mortons as we waited for the ferry to depart. It wasn't true: I had a master's in public health, which my mother liked to think of as a stepping-stone to medical school rather than the beginning of a career in social work. When I told my father what I planned to do with my life, he told me not to blame him for the fact that I'd inherited my mother's en-thusiasm for impractical causes, but he sent me the money for the plane ticket.

"A doctor," said Nancy. "That's impressive. Perhaps some of your drive will rub off on Sarah. She has it in her head to go traipsing around the desert for a year."

I looked at Sarah with real interest for the first time. She was rolling her eyes and twisting a strand of hair around her finger so tightly that her fingertips were turning red. We were built similarly, tits so that anything you wore that wasn't a giant burlap sack bordered on obscene, but the resemblance ended there. She'd made a pillow out of her Vanderbilt sweatshirt and was resting against it, dangling one arm over the back edge of her seat.

"Cecilia has always been good with science," my mother said. "She gets that from her father's side. I'd wanted to look you up for years, but it was Cecilia and her tech smarts that found you. I never had much of a head for science."

My mother was basing my scientific excellence on a ribbon I won for growing hydroponic tomatoes in the seventh grade, though I'd subsequently nearly failed biochemistry and dropped physics altogether. My father was a food critic who had recently been berated by a molecular gastronomist for identifying liquid nitrogen as "smoke" in his review. My tech smarts consisted of having entered Nancy Morton's older brother's name into Google. In fairness to my mother, we had, both of us, grown up without the ability to type someone's name into the ether and receive an immediate report on their current whereabouts. I'd always known about her cousins, but only that year had it occurred to me that one of the great unanswerable questions of her life was now in fact answerable, and instantly at that. The internet did still feel like a kind of mysterious magic then, a new power we had all only recently been granted and were still learning to use. When I finally left the Bay fifteen years later—the nonprofit I worked for was shutting down and I was already barely able to keep up with my rent increases—I took a long walk through the hills and looked across the water at the city that tech rebuilt and tried to remember when I'd first seen it coming, when I'd remembered that all magic, all progress, has a price.

Even at the time, the magic I used to get us answers had a trace of the ominous: it turned out that Nancy's brother had been killed in a car crash three years earlier. Nancy and her family had been mentioned in the obituary. I'd offered my belated condolences and invited them down to meet us on one of the Alcatraz ferries. They lived farther north, in Sonoma, and after a brief hesitation she had agreed to drive down for the day.

"Well it was different then," Nancy said. "With girls and science. They didn't encourage us much, did they, Anne?"

"No," said my mother. "No, they didn't. Lots of things were different then."

An unsaid thing hung in the air for a moment. Ken Morton cleared his throat.

"So," he asked, "why Alcatraz? Lovely day for it, but kind of an odd choice."

"I was going to ask the same thing. Interesting place for a reunion. We've never been—just moved out here a few years ago and never got around to half the tours. I hear it's beautiful though."

My mother looked like she might cry. Without thinking, I moved closer to her. It hadn't occurred to me to tell them why I had invited them here specifically. I had assumed that they would know.

"Didn't you know?" my mother asked. "That Papa was at Alcatraz? That that's why he—that's why things happened the way they did?"

A moment of surprise passed over Nancy's face, and then she collected herself.

"I had heard," she said slowly, "that he had done some time in prison, and was never really—never really right after that. I didn't know that it was Alcatraz. You know, I didn't get to know him that well. Not like you did."

"I guess you didn't," said my mother. "Nobody else did."

My mother sat on one of the benches on deck and hugged her arms to her chest. I sat down beside her. I could tell she was trying not to cry. I put an arm around her and patted her shoulder gently. The Mortons looked embarrassed to be there, and then turned away to watch San Francisco disappear from view.

. . .

Here is what you have to understand about my mother's childhood: it wasn't one. Her mother was the younger of Charlie and Louise's two children, both raised on the see-saw of his impractical excesses and her Yankee frugality. At sixteen, my grandmother ran off to join a theater; two years later she came back with a Black baby. She stayed home long enough to leave my mother in her parents' care and to meet a traveling salesman whom she ran off with a few months later. They never heard from her again. Some years later, the salesman sent a note with a copy of her obituary attached. When my mother was small, she and Papa would sit and make up stories about all the places her mother might be. Infinityland: somewhere north of Kansas, a place where you kept going and going but could never leave be-cause it was always getting bigger. Elfworld: somewhere in West Florida, where they kept shrinking you and shrink-ing you and you didn't realize you were an elf too until it was too late to do anything about it.

For years they lived together in the imaginary places, a world you could only be kept from by enchantment, but as soon as she was old enough, my mother left and kept going too, left that house and let the business of loving the man who raised her be confined to telephone calls from faraway places. It was a decision that probably saved her life, and one for which she never forgave herself. I didn't—and still don't—dare compare the terms of my life to my mother's, the stakes of my choices to hers, but I understand more now about how it feels to love the excess in people, about how knowing someone else's love will consume you doesn't make it any less real or any less reciprocated, about how you can leave a person behind just to save the thing they value most—yourself. Or maybe I understood it even then but couldn't have told you how.

· · ·

Here is what you have to understand about Charlie Sullivan: his life at home as a child was bad enough that joining the army at the tail end of World War I seemed like a safer and more cheerful alternative. At fifteen he falsified his birth certificate and enlisted. A captain decided he was too scrawny to be sent overseas. Instead, he was stationed as a border guard, where he spent his days looking backward toward California because his orders were to shoot anyone coming from Mexico, and he figured he couldn't shoot anyone if he didn't see them. They'd given him a gun that didn't work right anyway; it stuck sometimes when he tried to fire, which at first struck him as fortuitous. When it occurred to him that it might also be dangerous, he complained to a commanding officer, who told him if he wanted a real gun, he'd have to be a real soldier.

Stop complaining, they said, and so he did, until the night he was cleaning his gun and it fired accidentally, putting the same bullet through his best friend and an officer who'd been standing in the doorway. It had happened that quickly, the blast of the gun catching his friend in midlaugh, then silencing the commanding officer's scream. The first men to arrive at the scene had found Charlie sobbing over the body of his best friend, a nineteen-year-old kid from Jersey who wanted to be an architect. It wasn't until the base commander showed up that anyone even suggested he'd done it on purpose, but as soon as he did, Charlie was led off in handcuffs, and the previous reports of his gun malfunctioning vanished. They sent him to Alcatraz where he was convicted and sentenced to death by firing squad. They dragged him out of the basement for his execution twice, only to find it had been stalled. His appointed lawyer, an old army man who thought he'd seen enough evil to know what it wasn't, wouldn't retire until he got Charlie Sullivan out of prison. He managed to get sworn statements about my great-grandfather's faulty gun, his temperament and friendship with the deceased, the medical report that concluded one bullet had killed both men. It was enough to get him pardoned, though he was still dishonorably discharged. The army would admit only to procedural error.

When my mother left, he was alone with his ghosts. He didn't have my mother's patience for strategic approaches, didn't go through all the proper channels. He called and wrote letters to the Pentagon, trying to get his dishonorable discharge changed to an honorable one, trying to get the veterans' benefits he'd been demanding for forty years, trying to get a person instead of letterhead to answer him. He wrote to whom it may concern, but it concerned no one. When at last he got a personal response, a *We are very sorry but no*, from a Maj. Johnson somewhere, he dressed himself in a uniform he'd bought from an army surplus store, stood in the living room, and shot himself in the head.

My mother was a junior in college then, already engaged to my father. She spent money they had saved for her wedding to have him buried properly. It was nothing glitzy, no velvet and mahogany, but there was a coffin and a church service. My mother and a sprinkling of neighbors came to pay their last respects. Nancy's father was shamed into his Sunday best. He brought his children, including Nancy, but not his wife. They sat on the opposite side of a half-empty church. They didn't speak.

· · ·

When I am angry at my mother sometimes, I tell myself this story. If you really want to know what the six of us were doing on a boat to Alcatraz, here is what you need to understand about me: at eighteen I'd joined a college literary club, whereupon we came up with the brilliant idea of tattooing ourselves with quotations from our favorite authors.

Mine says *The past isn't dead. It isn't even past.* Growing up I watched my mother's every strategic move with some mixture of awe and resentment. I watched her stand up to lawyers who were better dressed and better paid, to imposing men in uniform, to friends who begged her to let the whole thing go already. I wondered sometimes where she got the strength for battle after battle, but more often than not she answered my question for me. After setbacks it was my comfort she sought, my hand she held, and for every word of encouragement I gave her I found myself swallowing the bitter declaration that I had never signed up for any of this—not the paperwork, not the support, not the faith in the ultimate benevolence of the universe that she seemed to take for granted that I shared with her. And yet, faith like that is contagious: I greeted her plans to spend the money she thought was coming to us by donating a bench in her grandfather's name to the city park with the wary reminder that we had no money coming to us yet; still I pictured him smiling down at us as we sat on it, the first generation in the family to achieve some semblance of peace. I rolled my eyes at my mother's occasional fantasy of being sought out by her missing cousins, but I memorized their names in case I ever ran into them, regularly looked over my shoulder and peered into the faces of strangers to see if I could map out any family resemblance.

Looking at them on the boat I'd summoned them to, I realized I never would have known them by sight; they looked like any other strangers. After my mother's revelation, the gulf between our families seemed even bigger than it had been when we'd met at the pier. The Mortons didn't talk much the whole rest of the boat ride, not even to each other. I sat by my mother and kept rubbing her shoulder.

"This could still work out," I said, even though I didn't know anymore what was supposed to be working.

·   ·   ·

Alcatraz loomed over us all, stony and angular with patches of green. My mother made halting conversation with Nancy. A woman in front of us pointed enthusiastically at the military barracks ahead. I looked up—rows and rows of matching windows, peeling paint that might have been white once. An old U.S. penitentiary sign had been affixed to the building over the WELCOME INDIANS graffiti that no one had painted over. All that history, bleeding into itself in the wrong order. Sarah was standing beside me, focused on the same sign. She fished through her shoulder bag and emerged with a tin of mints; I took one when she offered it and chewed, feeling the little bits of blue crystal grind against my teeth.

"Would you mind telling me what the hell is going on here?" she asked.

"At this point your guess is as good as mine," I said.

"I thought this was going to be a joke or something,"

Sarah continued. "I mean, who has long-lost relatives any-more?"

"Didn't you know about us?" I asked. I had known about them for as long as I could remember.

"Not really. My mom was never that close to her par-ents. We saw them like every other Thanksgiving. Less than that once my uncle died. And then they died too. We don't really even talk about them that much. Mom's been weird lately. I think she was happy to get the call. Dad thinks this whole thing is a bad idea. FYI, he thinks you're going to ask for money or something."

"Oh," I said. "Well we're not."

"Didn't think so." She stopped to examine a purple flower on a bush, then snapped it off and twisted it be-tween her fingers, staining them lavender. "My mom said something about a lawsuit."

"It's over. And anyway, it was never about the money. It was about the fact that he never should have been here."

I told her the story my mother had told me, the faulty gun, the death of his friends, the rats, his suicide.

"Fuck," she said, and we were quiet the rest of the way up.

. . .

When we caught up with our parents, I found my mother still listing slightly exaggerated versions of my accomplish-ments. It was the kind of subtle inflation of the truth you'd find in a family's annual holiday newsletter, but it made me angry. It wasn't that I doubted she was proud of me—her faith in me, I knew, was boundless. It was their faith in me she didn't trust, and I didn't like it, the way a group of strangers had the power to shake my mother's confidence. I had orchestrated the visit confident that my mother's cousin would be grateful for the chance to make amends, that she and her family would be eager to prove themselves better than the people who raised her. It had honestly not occurred to me that my mother and I would have to make a case for ourselves, that conditions could possibly be such that we were the ones who were supposed to impress them.

"You don't have to treat them like they're visiting royalty," I muttered to my mother as we approached the entrance of the main prison building. "They're just people."

"I'm treating them like they're people. They aren't props, Cecilia. You can't just order them to show up and expect the rest to take care of itself. But don't worry, keep up the attitude and no amount of convincing will make them like you. Be exactly what they were expecting, if that makes you happy."

I sulked behind my mother as we collected our headphones and prepared for the tour. The main prison building was dim, dingy, with anachronistically fresh green and gray paint. We walked into a room of mock visiting windows, glass with holes cut out for human contact. A small girl in pink overalls sat at one of the windows, tapping the glass and frowning at the dead black telephone she held against her ear, seeming genuinely confused by the absence of a voice on the other end. My mother took a breath and walked through the entryway. Rows and rows of prison bars greeted us. A family in front of us stretched out their souvenir map and tried to locate Al Capone's cell. I put one side of my headset over my ear and let the other headphone rest just behind the other ear, in case I needed to hear something more interesting. What I heard was Kelli.

"*Eewwwwww,*" she said to the exposed cell toilet, littered with tourist trash: cigarette butts and crumpled pieces of paper.

"Shut up and stop being an idiot, Kelli," said Sarah, which I appreciated until it was silent because no one could think of anything to say that wasn't idiotic. I put both headphones over my ears. *You are entitled to food, clothing, shelter, and medical attention. Everything else is a privilege.* I examined a scuff mark on the floor, noted how many people must have walked over this same ground, paid for the luxury of being reminded what privileges were. I tried to imagine what it would be like to live underneath it. *Turn left to see the gun gallery*, my audio guide informed me, then provided me with the sound of a smattering of rifle fire *rat-a-tat-tat*, in case, I suppose, I didn't know what a gun was.

I did know, and I knew my mother did too, knew she'd replayed Papa's last minutes over and over again in her head.

I had sat with her when she woke up screaming from night-mares about it, or from the old nightmare, the one she in-herited from him, the bullet flying from his gun, ripping through his bunkmate, going straight through whoever else appeared in the dream and tried to stop it. She kept the gun he shot himself with. It was locked in a case in our basement somewhere, unloaded. I had my own nightmares sometimes. I slept quietly, but not well. Lately I'd been dreaming I got a phone call like my mother had. I'd been having her night-mare, only this time it was her with the gun to her head, and I never woke up in time to save her.

Nothing was working out the way I'd wanted it to. Ken Morton was still walking around with his hands in his pockets, looking like he'd rather be anywhere else. Nancy Morton and my mother were still making tentative small talk about Sarah and Kelli and me and the weather. Kelli had surreptitiously placed her iPod earbuds under the audio tour headphones and was humming a pop song and making eyes at a spiky-haired boy who was taking the tour with his family. Sarah had pulled out a notebook. I tried to peer over her shoulder to read it, but her handwriting was illegible. No one was taking this seriously enough. Even the site itself seemed like a cheap approximation of the sacred ground I'd been expecting. It was more national park than any-thing else, dozens of people with sunglasses in their pock-ets clutching souvenir photos of themselves in the mock gallows and checking their watches to make sure they had left enough time for a picnic lunch. *Loud talking, shouting, whistling, singing, or other unnecessary noises are prohibited,* said the automated tour guide. I took my headphones off altogether. Kids ran by, giggling, their parents calling after them. A group of women in matching purple sun visors kept loudly asking questions of one another although it was clear none of them knew the answers.

My mother paused in front of one of the restored jail cells, and the rest of us stopped behind her. She slid the headphones off of her ears and walked in. Nancy followed her. Even with just the two of them, it was crowded, but Sarah and I squeezed in behind them anyway. Under the circumstances, neither of us quite trusted our mothers to their own devices.

"Tight squeeze," said Nancy. "Can you even imagine living in here?"

My mother opened and shut her mouth, but no words came out. I could see in her eyes the first of the tears I'd been expecting since she'd lost the appeal, the practiced composure of the past few weeks slipping from her. She sat on the floor of the cell and began to weep, shielding her perfectly made-up face with her hands. Ken Morton, who was still standing awkwardly outside the cell gate, took Kelli's hand and led her away. I tried to push past Nancy to sit beside my mother and hold her hand, but Nancy sat down beside her first, and let her cry. Sarah tugged at my sleeve, but I didn't go anywhere. I felt that the whole escapade was my mistake, and I'd be damned if I was going to let my mother's family screw her up again on my watch.

"That was stupid of me," said Nancy. She put a hand on my mother's shoulder. "Of course you've imagined."

My mother had stopped crying, but she didn't respond.

"I wanted to say something, you know," said Nancy. "At the funeral. I saw you sitting by yourself and I knew right away who you were, and I wanted to speak."

"But you didn't," said my mother, the edge I'd missed in her since she'd arrived in San Francisco finally creeping back into her voice. "You didn't even say hello."

"I was young," she said.

"I was younger," said my mother. "You were the only family I had left when he died. I thought his reputation would matter to you, like it did to me. He was your grandfather too."

"Not in the same way he was yours," said Nancy. "And I can't change that. It took me years to understand why my mother reacted to you the way she did, and when I did, I was ashamed, but I was still her daughter. There was a lot of sorting out to do. I do think she changed some. I think she regretted some of it. I know I did."

"At least you know what you regret. I'm forty-seven years old and after everything, Cecilia is all I've got."

"That's not true," I said, even though I had believed it all my life.

"Sometimes I think I know how Papa felt—I mean," she

said, noting my alarm, "not that I'd ever want to end it the way he did. Just that I don't know what there is left to try."

I looked at the metal bars, the scratches and fingerprints on them, the open doorway on the other side. How easy it was to feel stuck; how easy it was to walk out.

"There's this," Sarah said finally.

"There's this," my mother repeated, in a voice somewhere between a laugh and a sob. From farther down the hall, tourists were gawking at us. Nancy wrapped a protective arm around my mother, who leaned into her shoulder. Sarah grabbed my arm as she stepped away, and I walked out with her, accepting that it was time to let our mothers cry. I was unaccustomed to that then—to leaving while my mother was in need of comfort, to trusting anyone else to know what to do. I let myself be led away because Sarah seemed confident it was possible.

In the museum store, Kelli was laughing and dangling a pair of souvenir handcuffs just out of reach of the spiky-haired boy. Ken Morton was outside already, smoking a cigarette. He nodded in our general direction and went back to his smoking. This, I thought, was one of those times it would be easier to be male, or a smoker, to have a ready excuse to remove myself from emotional proceedings without anyone making an issue of it. Sarah pulled the mints out of her purse again and offered me one. She kept snapping the container open and shut.

"Mom hasn't been the same since my uncle died," said

Sarah. "It wasn't even that they were super close, just that he was what she had in the world, you know? Kelli is a godawful pain in the ass, but if anything happened to her, I'd be a wreck. I think that was why she was so excited to meet your mom. She liked the idea of having more family again. It might be good, if they can be friends."

"If," I said.

"It could happen," said Sarah. "Nothing like a prison to give you faith in humanity."

"A prison with a souvenir penny press," I said.

I looked around at all of the things for sale. Chocolate bars in Alcatraz wrapping. Posters with blown-up versions of prison regulations: #21. WORK. YOU ARE REQUIRED TO WORK AT WHATEVER YOU ARE TOLD TO DO. Along the wall a row of bronze cast keys were each engraved with cell numbers. I lifted one up with my finger for Sarah to see.

"Who buys these?" I asked. "Who walks in here and says this, this is what I need?"

"People who don't know what they need in the first place," she said. "So, pretty much anybody."

I considered this. I wondered how much I'd have to steal for it to equal $227,035.87. It seemed strange to me to have the number in my head then, and though it would never stop seeming strange to me, I kept the running tally for years after that afternoon, did the math annually, out of habit, even after my mother had stopped requesting it, even after I had stopped thinking of the world as a place that kept track of what it owed people, even after I stopped thinking of myself as a person who had the power to make demands of the world and learned to be a person who came up with her own small daily answers like everyone else. There was something comforting about imagining I knew exactly what I'd been cheated out of.

WHEN MY MOTHER AND NANCY emerged into the gift shop, their eyes were dry. There was something girlish in the way my mother came over to me, lighter after the cathartic tears. I tapped a key absentmindedly and it bumped the others; they jingled like wind chimes.

"We missed the three o'clock ferry," I told her.

"Did we?" she said, ruffling her fingers through my hair. "I think we'll live, kiddo. Let's hang out for a while."

I watched her walk out with Nancy Morton. The sun was hazy and insistent, and everyone seemed to shimmer as they stepped outside. I watched them walk away, and I had the feeling I was watching something heavy miraculously float.

In the years that followed, we would try two more holidays with the Mortons before the efforts were suspended indefinitely, victim to all of us being busy and, frankly, happier on our own. When we were alone after the final visit, my mother would confide in me that after all that, Nancy Morton had grown up to be boring. When my mother accepted that the legal system wouldn't give her justice, she said she would write a book about Papa's story, and while I heard about it for years, I never saw a manuscript. Sarah and I began a correspondence that started earnest and effusive, but tapered off, until eventually the extent of our relationship was me clicking like on her family photographs, not remembering which of her children was named what, her once commenting "Congratulations, I must have missed this!" when I was tagged in a photograph with two of the children I worked with, me intending but never bothering to correct her assumption they were mine.

That afternoon at Alcatraz we were all together, and I didn't know whether I had managed anything good or permanent or healing in gathering us there, only that it had previously been impossible. I slipped a bronze key off of its hook and closed it into my palm. I wanted someone to stop me or I wanted someone to tell me it was mine. I squeezed the key into my palm and walked out without anyone noticing. I walked into the glare of the light, down to the picnic tables near the water, where my family was gathered and laughing. I called to Sarah. I held the key out in my open palm and went to show my cousin what I'd done.

Why Won't Women Just Say What They Want

Everyone had heard that the genius artist had gone to some deserted island, to finish a project, or to start a project, or to clear his head, or to get away from some drama. People heard he had gone, and then no one heard anything for long enough that it became boring to speculate, until it had been so long it became curious again. The running joke about the volcano started when a reporter asked the Model/Actress Who Dated Him a While Ago what she thought the artist was up to, and she said, "Who knows? Who cares? I hope he fell into a volcano." At cocktail parties that spring, someone would ask where he was and someone else would say "Volcano" and laugh, until it was summer and the artist had been gone so long that people started to wonder if he had, in fact, met some violent and tragic end, and whether someone should be looking for him. Once upon a time any woman in his life would have hiked through lava for him, but by the time he left he had worn out his goodwill to the point that it would have been asking a lot of any one of them to so much as go run him an errand at the corner store.

When the apologies began, they were public and simultaneous. It was late summer, and they appeared suddenly and all at once, like brief afternoon thunderstorms. The High School Sweetheart's apology came over the PA system at the grocery store where she was buying bread and cheese, because her husband had promised to take care of shopping for the week but had, for some reason, come home with only deli meat and marinara sauce. The Model/Actress's apology came on billboards downtown in the city where she lived. The Long-Suffering Ex-wife's came as a short film projected on a giant screen in the park nearest the house where she lived with their daughter. It played in a loop until the city took it down. The Daughter's apology was posted on Instagram, marked with all of her frequently used hashtags. The On-Again Off-Again Ex of His Wayward Youth walked out of her apartment one morning, and by the time she returned at night, she found that the abandoned storefront next door had opened as a pop-up bar named after her, with her apology painted on the walls.

The apologies sounded like him and they did not sound

like him. They used correct and known-only-privately pet names. They contained details the wronged parties had carried quietly for years. They used phrases he would use. But they were unlike him in that they were, in fact, actual apologies, and in that way bore no resemblance to his previous efforts at making amends, which had all gone more or less like this:

To the Long-Suffering Ex-wife, a three-page typewriter-typed letter that used the words "I'm sorry" exactly once, in its conclusion, in the context "I've done the best I can here and I'm sorry if even after my attempt to apologize, you are unable to forgive me, although I have, clearly, forgiven you for giving up on me in the first place."

To the Former Personal Assistant, two apologies, first, in the middle of everything, a terse email that she knew even then to keep in her in-box forever: "It was a mistake to have sex with you again and I'm sorry you got hurt," and then, years later, well after she was no longer anyone's personal assistant, and shortly after she'd turned down working an event because he'd be one of the presenters, a second apology, via the Soon-to-Be Short-Suffering Second Ex-wife, who cornered her at a gala and said, "He says to tell you he's sorry about whatever's going on in your life, but you need to stop making shit up about him when he barely remembers you and never touched you."

To the Short-Suffering Second Ex-wife, just before the divorce, in a chain of text messages:

The Artist: I do concede that I owe you an apology for the way that I phrased things. There was probably a kinder way to express my frustration with your unreasonable expectations than to say that you just didn't understand why so many women I had history with were still in my life because you'd never known what it was like to be as successful as I am, and, as a woman, in order to understand it, you'd have to imagine what things would be like for you if you were beautiful. But it's unfair of you to accuse me of being cruel to you in public when we were not in public. We were, for the record, in a crowded bar.

TSSEW: WTF? A crowded bar is literally the definition of public. How can that not be public? If you were making a book about places to have fights, a crowded bar would be the textbook definition of "in public."

The Artist: Well, I was hoping to leave things amicably, but if you're going to be childish and condescending like this, then we clearly can't have a reasonable conversation.

To the Daughter, a note slipped under the door she'd locked herself behind while visiting him for the summer. It read "I understand it was upsetting for you to find out this way, but 'SAT tutor' is not a proprietary relationship; she is not *your* SAT tutor in the sense of *belonging* to you, and there's no reason for you to be so upset about our relationship, or to compare it at all to Shannon, who I'm sorry is no longer your friend, but, I remind you, was redshirted in kindergarten because her parents didn't want her to mature late, and is a year older than you, and was eighteen when I asked her out, which I'm sorry made her uncomfortable, but reasonably assumed was what she wanted at the time." It was signed "Love, Dad," with a hand-drawn smiley face.

Now he was sorry without caveat or redirection. He was sorry without taking the opportunity to tell a long story about the things that had brought him to this point, a story causing the person whom he was supposed to be comforting to comfort him instead. He was sorry in specific and concrete ways. He was sorry about the time he cost the Former Personal Assistant a job by off-the-record calling her a crazy bitch, and sorry for lying to her face about it. He was sorry for telling the Short-Suffering Second Ex-wife that things were over with the Long-Suffering Ex-wife when in fact he was still fucking her most nights and fighting with her most mornings. He was sorry he'd said that thing about the Model/Actress's mother, and also sorry he'd said that thing about the left side of the Model/Actress's face, which was really exactly like the right side and perfectly lovely. He was sorry for telling the Long-Suffering Ex-wife that she was lucky she'd met him when she had because she had never been good enough for him, and if they'd met a year later he would have already known that. He was sorry for bringing the Daughter along and seating her beside him on multiple occasions when he was afraid a woman would otherwise yell at him, sorry for teaching her that however much he loved her, she was still a tool for him to use. He was sorry about the time he'd playfully squeezed a hand around the High School Sweetheart's throat and kept it there well past the point where her eyes showed a flicker of real fear, because he could, and then removed it and laughed and said, "What, you don't trust me?" He was sorry for the time he argued with the On-Again Off-Again Ex of His Wayward Youth and gripped her arm so hard he left a bruise, and sorrier still for insisting, when she pointed to it the next day, that the bruise wasn't there and she was seeing things. He was so sorry for everything.

THE LONG-SUFFERING EX-WIFE thought that perhaps the apologies were his latest art project. It made her nervous and upset to think of him watching for a reaction. She hired a private detective to see if he had cameras on her somehow, but nothing turned up.

The High School Sweetheart went home from the store and hugged her children and kissed the mouth of her husband who had forgotten all the important groceries, and tried to remember what being dramatically wounded by the artist had felt like, but found that she could not, that when she tried to find the words to explain to her husband the things the artist had said and done to her and now finally apologized for, she was describing some other person's ugly life, a life that did not belong in her kitchen. She left the groceries sitting on the counter and went to have a glass of wine in the living room. When she came back, her husband had put the groceries away, and had lasagna in the oven, and their teenager was at the table doing homework and humming along with her headphones, and she almost cried at how stupid she'd been all that time ago, feeling bereft when the artist went off into the world without her.

The On-Again Off-Again Ex of His Wayward Youth spun in circles in the pop-up bar to read her apology and wondered if it would have meant something to get it two decades earlier, if she would have been a different and kinder person if she hadn't believed it when he told her that she was too smart to want kindness over honesty and she would never have both, if she hadn't learned so young that you could wring yourself out on someone's front lawn, and even after everything he'd said about you being the muse, the spark, the reason for it all, he could shut the window, could not just not love you, but not even really see you.

She thought if the artist could make amends, then any-one could, so she called the married man she was sleeping with and canceled their vacation, then called the man she'd once left for the artist years ago and said she owed him an apology, at which point he reminded her that she'd already apologized specifically and profusely years ago, and he did not forgive her then or now. She texted a paragraph of urgent feelings to the man she'd wished she'd left the art-ist for, who had moved on by the time the artist left her, and he texted back Who is this? The next day she called back the married man and told him to uncancel their vaca-tion, which he'd never canceled in the first place.

The Model/Actress called her marketing people to see if her makeup line could get a volcano-themed fragrance and makeup palette in stores for the fall season. Once they covered the obvious reddish and orangey and brown colors, they rounded things out with a near-black shade called Mol-ten, a light gray called Ash Cloud, and a shimmery white they renamed Rhyolite, after the team decided Pompeii was too morbid.

The Short-Suffering Second Ex-wife wanted to com-miserate and compare notes, and so she reached out to the Long-Suffering Ex-wife, who did not take her calls because in her mind the Short-Suffering Second Ex-wife would al-ways be the Mistress Who Was Dumb Enough to Actu-ally Marry Him and Deserved What She Got.

The Daughter took the Short-Suffering Second Ex-wife's call and met her for coffee. The Daughter called Shannon and invited her for a drink at the bar that didn't card any-one. Shannon didn't come. The Daughter had many drinks and took a car service to the home of the Short-Suffering Second Ex-wife, so her mother would not see her, and passed out on the couch. *Why are you like this?* the Daughter wanted to ask everyone involved, but she sensed on some level that the question would be hypocritical, that she too was like something, and just didn't know what yet.

The Former Personal Assistant holed up in her penthouse apartment and summoned her own personal assistant to bring her good bourbon and ripe oranges, and wept, and read and read and read her apology, which was in the form of one of those mindless point-and-click phone app games she used to play when she was bored during travel. It gave her a new apology for every hidden object she found. When she was certain she'd found them all, she turned her phone off to resist the temptation to write to everyone who'd ever met her account of him with even a flicker of doubt and say, "Did you see it? Did you see I was telling the truth?" because what was this whole life she'd built if not already a way of telling anyone who'd ever doubted anything about her to fuck off?

After the first round, the apologies became less extensive but grew in number and degree of precision. He apologized to:

The Girl He Did Know Was Blackout Drunk Because He Was Actually Mostly Sober

The Girl Who Was So Stunned by Her Apology That It Sent Her to Therapy Because She Had No Recollection of Meeting Him, Let Alone Having Sex with Him

The Girl He Knew Was Only Pretending to Like It Rough
Because She Wanted to Make Him Happy but Said Nothing
to Because He Liked Making Her Pretend to Like It

The Girl Who Really Did Like It Rough, Who Was Annoyingly
Undiminished by Her Pleasure Until He Told Her Nobody
Would Ever Really Love Her Because She Was Such a Whore

The Guy He Made Homophobic Jokes About in College but Still
Asked to Suck Him Off Sometimes

The Closeted Friend He Never Touched but Whose Longing
He Nevertheless Made as Much Use of as He Would Have
Any Woman's

Shannon

The Intern Who Left the Art World After Their Summer Fling

The Woman He Asked to Back Out of a Grant They Were Both
Up For and Ended Things with as Soon as She Did

The Model Whose Breast He Grabbed Once as a Joke

The Girl Who Wondered All Those Years What to Call What Had
Happened Between Them Because Yeah She Had Intended to
Have Sex with Him but She Hadn't Intended It to Happen Like
That and She Hadn't Expected Him to Hurt Her but Not Notice
or Care or Stop

After those apologies were done, he doubled back on
the first round of apologies, the latest revelations having

made necessary some addenda. He was sorry for the year he'd driven the Long-Suffering Ex-wife to experimental therapy for delusional anxiety, after convincing her that her insecurity was making it impossible for him to love her and she'd entirely invented his flings with the Intern and the Girl He Knew Was Only Pretending. He was sorry about the time he told the Former Personal Assistant she was stupid and bad at her job when she correctly accused him of tasking her with calendaring his dates with the Girl Who Really Did Like It Rough and pretending they were work events. He was so sorry.

He was sorry and he was sorry and he was sorry, and then he was back. Maybe he'd never gone anywhere. No one could remember anymore why they'd all been so certain there had been a deserted island. Now there was a gallery. No one knew quite what was in it. The apologies, they guessed. But what else? The show was called *Forgiveness*. He invited the critics. He invited everyone he'd apologized to.

The Long-Suffering Ex-wife felt vindicated by her suspicion that this had been some kind of publicity stunt and refused to participate. The Daughter was embarrassed by the thought of being in a room with her father and a cloud of women he had treated badly, though she couldn't say for certain whether she was embarrassed by him or for him. The On-Again Off-Again Ex of His Wayward Youth was on her uncanceled vacation in Paris with her lover's tongue between her legs. The Short-Suffering Second Ex-wife thought it would be embarrassing to go if the first wife wasn't going to bother. The Model/Actress intended to show up late and make an entrance. The Former Personal Assistant imagined being forced to hug him in front of a crowd and swore not to go, and then imagined the feeling she'd have hugging him, especially if he looked into her eyes and said he was sorry, and thought she might go after all, and RSVP'd, and then, standing in front of the mirror looking at herself in a cocktail dress the day of, remembered that when he'd left her for the last time—brokenhearted and unemployed!—he had left her curled up sobbing in a ball on her kitchen floor, remembered that whole horrid year after, the year before she clawed her way out of that life and into this one. She took off the dress, and called a friend who also remembered that year, and so sat in the Former Personal Assistant's living room for hours blocking the front door of her apartment in case she got it in her head to change her mind.

THE GALLERY was three large rooms. In the first, the films played, projected against one wall, while the pop-up bar, complete with drinks and bartenders, was reproduced along the wall opposite. In the second room, the app was available on a touchscreen, and pictures of the billboards in their original context had been framed and mounted.

In the bathrooms, in case anyone became overwhelmed by their personal apology and needed a minute, there were thoughtful but generic apologies carved into the mirror glass and printed on the tissues.

The third room contained the mouth of a volcano. It looked to be made of ice but gave off real smoke. There was a short staircase leading to a platform at the volcano's lip. The artist stood on the platform. The point of the volcano room, said a sign at the entrance, was that if anyone was unsatisfied with his apology, he would keep trying. If anyone came into the room still wanting him inside of a volcano, he would not leave until he got it right. If he made it worse, he should be pushed in.

There were more critics and arts-and-culture writers in the gallery than apology recipients, and those who bothered to show up had mostly made their peace. The artist stood quietly on the platform near the volcano for nearly an hour. Shannon came into the volcano room and yelled at him and he consoled her; it was easy, he had, after all, known her since she was a child. The Model/Actress's limo circled the block, waiting for the right moment of entrance while her people debated which angle of entry had the best natural light for her to walk in. The Girl Who Was So Stunned by Her Apology It Sent Her to Therapy walked in and out of the gallery several times, trying to find the right words for her question but never did and left without asking it.

The Girl Who Had Wondered All These Years What to

Call It watched the artist apologize to Shannon, and when Shannon left, she came up to the platform. It took the artist a moment to recognize her, and when he did he was soft with her, but he could not explain what he had done to her and neither could she, and it felt unfair to her that she should have to find the words. He had apologized already for causing her pain. He had apologized already for ignoring her pain when he knew it was there, because he'd been an ass and his pleasure existed independent of it. But now he fumbled for what was left to be sorry for. He was sorry he hadn't been kinder the morning after? He was sorry he'd been too kind the night before and made himself seem like a different type of man? He was sorry she didn't get what she wanted? What had she wanted? She had the same feeling she'd had when he unceremoniously handed her back her underwear. Like it was a technicality that she hadn't specifically told him she wanted to be treated like a person. She came closer. She pushed. When he fell, everyone waited for his reemergence. It did not come. Security ushered people out of the gallery. An ambulance came. The volcano had a pit of hot liquid. No one but the artist had known exactly what was inside. It was not literally lava, but might as well have been. They tried to pull him out. It was too late. It had been too late immediately.

The On-Again Off-Again Ex of His Wayward Youth thought it was carelessness, that the artist had always been more about vision than details, that, truthfully, some of his art was brilliant but much of it had always been sloppy, and he'd probably been more concerned that the lava look right than that it be safe to fall into or give him time to get out. The Long-Suffering Ex-wife and the Short-Suffering Second Ex-wife both thought he'd planned it this way, to go out on his own terms and still make it someone else's fault. The Girl Who Had Wondered All These Years What to Call It did not know what to think and did not face charges, but she spent the next few years in and out of hospitals. The High School Sweetheart never thought of him again. The Former Personal Assistant thought maybe he'd been supposed to find a grip or foothold on the inside somewhere, but had slipped. The Daughter thought he might have staged it, that there might have been a trick exit somewhere. Quietly she waited years, well into her adulthood, for him to come back and tell her how it worked.

The Model/Actress knew: the volcano was dangerous because he'd never actually expected to be in it. He had always counted on being good enough in the end. He had counted on absolution. He had counted on love. "Thank you," he was going to say when everyone was appeased, while he stood on the platform and dramatically revealed the volcano's violent core. "Your generosity tonight has saved my life again." He thought the *Forgiveness* was his to declare. It was right there in the title.

The Model/Actress called her marketing people about canceling the volcano product launch and figuring out how to repackage and rebrand the makeup that was already in warehouses. Marketing called back and said that preorders were actually up, and they could take the loss if she felt sentimental about it in light of recent events, but as a limited-edition line it was poised to sell out. The Model/Actress went to the memorial service in a tasteful smoky eye. They were going forward with the launch because what better way to honor the man who taught her how to really see color, she said. Plus, marketing said, everyone could see now that the makeup was tear proof.

It sounded calculated, but she really had cried. Afterward, someone asked the Model/Actress why she'd ever said volcano in the first place, and whether she felt at all responsible for planting the suggestion. The Model/Actress thought she had probably said volcano because sometimes when she thought of him she thought of burning. The local opera had been doing *Dido and Aeneas* the winter they were last together, and after he left her, and after the after, when she asked him to say sorry, and he said he was sorry they'd ever met, she thought all the time of Dido, Queen of Carthage, and her funeral pyre. For months she dreamed of showing up at one of his shows to light herself on fire and make him clean up the mess.

The year they were together, back when he was only moderately famous and she was nobody, he had asked her what she wanted out of life and she told him, because she didn't yet know any better than to say the truth, which was that she wanted everything. He kissed her forehead and said, "My little lady of ruthless ambition." In the months after that, he would sometimes ask her "How's conquering the world going, my sweet ruthless girl?" in the delighted dumbed-down tone you would use to tell a house pet it was ferocious. She would nuzzle him, beginning to understand that just because he didn't see something in her didn't mean it wasn't there, knowing there was still some freedom in the way he did not fathom yet how real and how necessary her ruthlessness would be.

Anything Could Disappear

Vera was moving to New York on a Greyhound bus, carrying only a duffel bag. The morning she left Missouri, there was a heat advisory and an orange-level terrorism alert. An hour outside of Chicago, there had been an older woman, crying and demanding that the bus pull over to let her off. From Chicago to Cleveland, she had sat next to a perfectly cordial man who had just finished a ten-year prison sentence and was on his way home from Texas with nothing but his bus ticket and twenty dollars in his pocket. Between Cleveland and Pittsburgh, there had been a man who kept trying to get her to share a blanket with him, citing their proximity to the air-conditioning vent, and between Pittsburgh and Philly, a teenage runaway had sat beside her and talked her ear off. And now there was this: a small, wobbly child whose mother had deposited him in the seat beside her with a simple "Keep an eye on him, will ya, hon?"

Vera tried to catch the eye of another passenger, maybe the woman two seats ahead of her on the other side of the aisle—she looked like the sort of person who would turn around and say, *Keep an eye on him your damn self, lady; he's yours, ain't he?*—but nobody looked up. The boy was around two years old, brown-skinned with a head of curls that someone had taken the time to properly comb. He was dressed in a clean, bright red T-shirt, baby jeans, and sneakers nicer than Vera's. The mother was a thin, nervous white woman, with wispy hair in three shades of blond. She smelled strongly of cigarette smoke and chocolate milk. She had gotten on the bus with the boy and a girl, about seven, who looked like her in miniature. The little girl was chewing purple bubble gum with the kind of enthusiasm that would have prompted Vera's own mother to ask, "Are you a young lady or a cow?" The mother had a cell phone pressed to her ear and was having a terse conversation with someone on the other end. She kept the phone cradled between her ear and shoulder, even as she leaned over the baby to kiss him on the forehead before walking farther toward the back of the bus.

"I feed him, don't I?" she said into the cell phone. "When was the last time you did?"

The little boy made Vera nervous. He was a quiet, happy baby. He would occasionally clap his hands together, applauding something only he could appreciate. Still, he was so small. Vera was overcome by the unreasonable belief that he might break if she looked away from him. As she watched him, he seemed to be watching her back. In the window on the other side of the boy, Vera could see her own hazy reflection, nothing to write home about one way or the other. She had been on buses, at that point, for sixteen of the last twenty-one hours. She was wearing jeans and an old T-shirt from the college she'd dropped out of two years earlier. Her hair was pulled back into a ponytail that was starting to frizz. Vera was a few months past her twenty-first birthday, which had happened without any of the fanfare and excess people tended to associate with turning twenty-one. Josh and her coworkers at the record store had ordered her a pizza at work and opened a few beers to toast her. That was it.

Somewhere on the Jersey Turnpike, the bus pulled into one of those rest stops that appeared up and down 95 like punctuation marks. Vera went into the travel plaza to get a cup of coffee. In the women's restroom, she stretched her arms above her head in the mirror and rolled up on the balls of her feet, then down again. She splashed water on her face, then pulled a small bottle of mouthwash from the duffel bag she'd carried in with her and swirled a capful around in her mouth before spitting into the sink.

When she got back on the bus, the little boy was still sitting in the seat beside her. Vera felt more charitably toward him now that she had seen how easy it was to walk away. She made faces at him that made him giggle. She tried to engage him in a game of patty-cake, but he seemed more interested in the clapping than the repetition.

When the bus finally pulled into Port Authority, Vera squeezed past the boy's seat to retrieve her duffel bag from the overhead bin. As she scrunched her face at the weight of the bag, the boy began to giggle again. She smiled back at him, then looked over her shoulder for his mother and sister. The people in the back of the bus were walking off one by one, but there was no sign of the blond woman or her daughter. Thinking maybe they'd somehow passed her already, Vera picked up the little boy, balancing him on her hip, and rushed off the bus, into the parking lot. No mother. She put the boy down and watched the rest of the passengers exit the bus, until it sat there, empty. Still no mother.

"Excuse me," Vera said to a heavyset older woman. "Did you see a blond woman and a little girl? They were just on the bus with us."

"Woman on the cell phone?"

"Yeah," said Vera.

"Think they got off in Jersey. Sounded like someone was supposed to meet her there." The woman grabbed her suitcase from beside the bus and walked off.

Vera looked around at the rapidly dispersing passengers, wondering what the hell was wrong with them that none of them had noticed a child being abandoned. But as she unintentionally tightened her grip on his hand, Vera realized that to the crowd it looked like he'd been her little boy all along. In the lazy American vernacular of appearances, Vera, with her color and hair that matched his, looked more like his mother or sister than his own mother and sister did. Had that been why the mother had chosen her? Maybe she'd intended to leave him all along. Or maybe something terrible had happened to her at the rest stop, she'd been dragged off by a stranger and was hoping someone would notice she was missing before it was too late. Or maybe she'd just gotten distracted, smoking a cigarette for too long, and was now frantic because the bus had left without her.

In any case, the obvious thing was to go to the police, to let them straighten the whole thing out. But there was this little boy, who was holding on to Vera with his left hand while he sucked the thumb on his right. And there was this duffel bag, where, between two layers of clothing, wrapped in a layer of plastic, and then a layer of gift wrap, Vera had carefully placed a package containing twenty thousand dollars' worth of cocaine. It was the last favor she was ever doing for Josh, and new as she was to this, she knew better than to walk into a police station with it.

"What's your name, sweetie?" Vera asked the little boy.

He shook his head. She scanned him for signs of a name tag, finally finding one on the inner lining of his T-shirt—someone had scrawled WILLIAM, in black Sharpie, on the tag inside.

"Come on, William," Vera said. "Let's get something to eat."

VERA TOOK HIM to a McDonald's and watched him nibble at his French fries and chicken nuggets. She considered dropping him off on the steps of a police station and just walking away, but that felt fraught with unsavory possibilities. He might follow her and get more lost than he already was. Someone might see her leaving him and try to stop her. There'd be more questions asked than she had answers for. She had one thousand dollars in cash tucked into the lining of her handbag, and when she went to drop this package off tomorrow she'd have ten thousand dollars more, and her whole life in front of her.

The year before she'd dropped out, she'd fulfilled her university's mandatory community service requirement by working with a literacy program at a women's prison. There were women not much older than she was doing ten years for holding, selling, transporting—mostly their boyfriends' drugs. A classmate said once that they'd bargained their lives for a few thousand dollars, which just emphasized for

Vera how much the classmate had missed the point—most of these women weren't getting money in the first place. They'd done it for love.

Fuck love. This was not a love story. Josh was in his late thirties, already balding and prone to wearing button-down Hawaiian print shirts. He'd half-heartedly hit on Vera once, but even he couldn't take the flirtation seriously enough to be offended by her rejection. He owned the record store, which had been a hardware store until his father died. For at least the last decade he'd been making more money selling pot and small-time quantities of pills out of the back room than he had selling records out of the front room; not because he'd started selling more drugs but because people had stopped buying music. Until now, Vera had strictly worked the front-room business, maintaining plausible deniability of whatever else her employer was doing. She kept a blank face while ringing up music of questionable taste, pornographic album covers, actual pornography, and cigarettes that twentysomething men purchased for the fourteen-year-old girls lingering outside. Vera got good at pretending not to notice people who didn't want to be seen.

The revival downtown had been promising her for years sputtered and stopped when the recession hit. Even after she'd dropped out of school, it had seemed better to stay put than to go an hour backward and end up at home again. Her father had suggested she get her cosmetology degree and work at the nail salon that had opened in town, and Vera said, *You want me to get a job literally watching paint dry?* When she called her parents back to apologize for her tone, she made it sound like Josh's store was really something and she had big plans, when in fact every day she felt like she had less energy to even imagine what better version of herself she might become.

Beneath the renovated downtown lofts that nobody had moved into were boarded-up windows that were supposed to be art galleries. The stoners who hung around the record shop were positively comforting in comparison to the kids who hung out in the downtown parking lots tweaking, flashing her the singed remainders of their teeth. Josh had refinanced the shop and then blew the money on a bad investment and had trouble paying the mortgage. Vera worked there for two years and made minimum wage the whole time. She had no savings and Josh knew it; he had more than once spotted her a twenty for lunch and dinner when it was close to payday and he saw she wasn't eating anything. Through someone he knew he'd gotten ahold of this drug, which was not meth, which was not heroin, which was a flittery thing, a onetime thing. He wasn't going to chance selling it in his own backyard—the cops had let him slide on the weed, but they were getting antsy. He knew a guy in New York though, and all she had to do was

get it there and she could take a fee. Josh would get out of
hot water with the lender, and she could get the hell out
of Missouri and not look back.

When William had finished eating, Vera took his hand
again and went outside to a pay phone. She called the phone
number she had seen on the side of a city bus, and made an
anonymous tip that a woman and a little girl may have
been hurt near exit 9 of the Jersey Turnpike. No, she didn't
know their names. No, she didn't know where they were
coming from or where they were going. No, she couldn't say
why she thought they might be in danger. No, she couldn't
stay on the line. She caught a cab, checked into a hotel, put
the baby to bed, and called her mother to tell her everything was fine.

IN THE MORNING, she took the train to the address Josh
had given her. She took William with her because she wasn't
sure what else to do with him. The building was unspectacular from the outside, a grim brownstone. She rang the
buzzer twice. On the second buzz, a female voice answered
and asked who it was.

"I'm Vera," she said. "Josh sent me."

The door buzzed open. Vera walked up the narrow stair-
well and opened the door in front of her. She thought at
first she must have written the number down wrong. She

was in an office—polished hardwood floors, bright accent colors on the walls, sunlight coming in through the loft windows, a sleek red couch, and a waiting area near a front desk. A woman with a blond-streaked ponytail sat behind it. A sign on the wall behind her read BROOKLYN DELIVERS.

"Can I help you?" she asked.

"I need to talk to Derek. My name's Vera."

The woman hit a button on the phone. A few seconds later, a man with short dreads and a T-shirt featuring a band she'd never heard of came out to greet her, a perplexed look on his face.

"I'm Vera," she said again.

Derek stared at William, who Vera had propped up on her hip.

"You brought a baby?" he asked.

"He's two," Vera said, as if this were an adequate explanation.

"Hold on." Derek disappeared into the back room, but before the door shut behind him, Vera could hear him say, "Who the fuck are we dealing with? He sent a girl with a kid."

A second man, this one with scruffy blond hair and thick black-framed glasses, came out of the room.

"I'm Adam," he said. "Josh sent you?"

"Yes," said Vera. She gestured toward William. "I'm sorry about him. I didn't know where else to leave him. I just got here yesterday."

"It's cool. You want to leave him out here for a minute? Liz can keep an eye on him."

Vera eyed the woman behind the desk. She hadn't looked up from the computer screen. Vera deposited William on the floor and followed Adam to the back room, which looked like a more posh version of the front room—hardwood floors, plush couches, walls of file cabinets.

"This is not what I was expecting," she said to Adam.

"We're a courier service," said Adam. "We deliver things. Mostly documents and packages for small businesses. Sometimes not."

"Oh," said Vera.

"You're not what we were expecting either," said Derek.

"Sorry," said Vera.

"I didn't say it was a bad thing. Just, Adam met Josh a while back on a road trip. From what he described, you don't really seem like the kind of girl he'd be hanging around with. That his kid?"

"No," said Vera.

"A woman of few words," said Adam. "It's a good instinct."

They finished their transaction quickly, without any of the sinister fanfare Vera had anticipated. Josh's money was wired. She put her cash in the bag where the drugs had been. She walked out to find William safely where she'd left him, and exited the building feeling an anticlimactic sense of relief.

VERA OPENED a bank account and deposited two thousand dollars. She sat in a coffee shop with William, calling through the rentals section on Craigslist. A few hours later, a Russian woman in Red Hook rented her an attic apartment. Vera had a list of friends willing to serve as fake landlord references, but the woman asked few questions once it became clear to her that Vera planned to pay both the first month's rent and the security deposit in cash. The first night in the apartment, they slept on the floor. She watched the rise and fall of William's chest, the delicate flaring of his tiny nostrils. *He'll need a bed*, she thought, and as soon as she thought it, she realized that the idea of giving him back had gone out the window. He would be hers unless and until someone took him away.

For the time being, William seemed like less trouble than anything else she'd gotten herself into. He was quiet, he was happy, and he imposed a certain order on her life. Meals had to be eaten at set times. There was bedtime, and time for waking up. Vera rented a U-Haul and picked up furniture around the city. When she went to buy a baby bed from a woman in Park Slope, the woman cooed over William and threw in a stroller for fifty bucks. By the end of the week, the apartment was in order and the money was half gone.

Vera had intended all along to look for a job once she

got here, but now there was the problem of having William. She couldn't very well take him along for interviews, or even to drop off résumés, because what if they wanted to talk to her then and there? Formal day care seemed likely to involve more paperwork than she currently possessed, which meant she'd need a babysitter, which meant she'd need to spend some time figuring out whom to trust with him. She felt a pang of guilt at her nervousness about leaving him with a stranger. After all, what was she? She googled "William," "missing child," and "New Jersey," setting the dates within the past month, and found no evidence that anyone was looking for him.

On Sunday, Vera took William for a walk in Prospect Park. She bought him an ice pop from one of the street vendors. While she sat in the grass with him, feeding him ice and singing, to the best of her abilities, "Little Bunny Foo Foo," she heard a voice call her name. She turned around to see the man with the short dreads approaching her.

"Vera, right?" he asked.

"Yeah," said Vera. "Derek?"

He nodded. "So you're sticking around?"

"Hopefully for good. I was just doing a favor on my way out here."

"Expensive favor."

Vera shrugged.

"So what's your son's name?"

"William," Vera answered without hesitation, though

she had not yet used the word *son* in reference to him. Derek sat down and began to play peekaboo with him.

"His dad around?"

"You see anyone but me around?"

"OK then," said Derek. William uncovered his face and looked disappointed that Derek had stopped playing with him. Derek reached out and tickled William's belly until he laughed his high-pitched baby giggle.

"You know anyone who's good with kids?" Vera asked.

"I'm not good enough?" Derek laughed. "I thought little man and I were getting along fine."

"I need someone to watch him," said Vera. "I need to find a job."

"What do you do?"

"I used to be a cashier."

"Just a cashier, or you kept records?"

"I kept records."

"You ever answer phones?"

"When they ring."

"Look," said Derek. "Our receptionist just quit. She's moving to LA. You interested? You answer phones, you file papers, you schedule pickups and deliveries, and ninety-five percent of what we do is legal."

"And the other five percent?"

"Is why you'd be making twenty dollars an hour instead of eleven. We try not to get in the middle of the messy stuff. We get everything in small quantities here and there and then we overcharge for it because there's a market of kids who want their drugs but are too lazy or scared to find their own dealer. We're middlemen, basically. Not even middlemen, because we don't even do that much buying straight from the source. We mostly stay under the radar."

"What about William?"

"As long as he doesn't fuss, you can bring him until you find someone to watch him."

William grinned, and then covered his mouth with his grape ice–stained fingers, as if to show how unfussy he could be.

SO JUST LIKE THAT, Vera's life fell into place, or out of it. She worked seven to four at the office, answering phones, filing papers, keeping two sets of books. She learned the last receptionist's filing system—the bike messengers without a *C* next to their names were only to carry documents and other innocuous packages for businesses that needed to get something from one part of the city to another before the end of the business day. The ones with a *C* could make both regular deliveries and irregular deliveries. She liked the messengers—they came in and out of the office to pick up assignments, packages, schedules, checks. They consulted with each other about the fastest routes and the best bike locks. They called her, sometimes, sheepish and lost in a city that some of them knew in their blood and others were perpetually perplexed by, even as they pretended that no address daunted them. They were her age, or even younger, and they all had something urgent to be doing with their lives, only it hadn't happened yet.

They competed against one another and their own personal bests to set records for transit time. They were paid by the number of deliveries they made. She could identify some of them by their scars—the accident scrapes and scratches or, in one case, the thin jagged line left by a bike thief's knife. Most of the messengers were oblivious to William's presence, but a few gave him candy if they had it or sat down on the floor and played with him while they waited for Vera to finish doing what they needed done. Since no one seemed fazed by William's presence in the office, least of all William, the idea of finding him a babysitter gradually faded away. One day she came into the office and found a playpen behind the desk, with a note on it from Adam and Derek, and the matter seemed settled.

Adam and Derek had grown on her. They were only a few years older than Vera was, but they seemed younger sometimes, both prone to fits of silliness and then mercurial sulking. They'd been friends since high school, somewhere in the Jersey suburbs, and sometimes they spoke their own language, comprised entirely of shared memories. They claimed to live untethered lives, apparently oblivious to how helpless they would each be without the other. Adam always left a coffee on Vera's desk in the morning.

Derek made her playlists or left her notes with her name drawn in fanciful script. A few years ago, Derek had been trying to start a graphic design business, about five years too late. Adam had been a bike messenger, who figured that if he were the person running things instead of the person delivering things, he could make more money without damn near killing himself in city traffic. Adam convinced Derek that he could turn his design business into a courier business if Adam went in for half, which, thanks to a loan from an uncle, he did. After a rough first year, they started splitting their business between legal and illegal goods, and three years later, here they were.

And now here was Vera, wiping her old life clean. She could have explained New York, probably even the job, maybe even the money, but there was no accounting for William. She deleted her Facebook page. She closed her old email account and opened a new one that only people who knew her now were aware of. She canceled her old cell phone service and bought a new phone. She called her mother once a week, using a phone card and a pay phone at the laundromat. *I'm fine,* she said, over and over again. *I love you. I don't know when I'm coming home to visit.*

William began to talk more, and Vera took a certain pride in hearing him say her name. He called her Ve-ra and not Ma-ma, which seemed only fair, and which she explained by telling people she'd felt too young to be anybody's mama when she had him. She read him bedtime stories at night and taught him his colors and letters. She had no one to ask how to do this right. At the first threat of snow, Derek bought him a winter hat, which Vera interpreted as part friendly gesture, part admonishment.

That night she gave William a bath with lilac baby soap. She washed his curly hair and his chubby body. He splashed in the bathtub.

"Are you happy?" Vera asked. "Am I taking good care of you?"

He flashed his baby teeth at her. Vera scooped him into a towel, dried, lotioned, and powdered him, and put him in his fleece pajamas. He fell asleep with his head nestled into the crook of her neck. Even as kids, some girls were about babies the way other girls were about bands or horses or witchcraft, but Vera had never been like that. Babies were loud and sticky, and part of why she'd started college in the first place was sex ed made it seem like it was one or the other—either you got a degree or an infant would be assigned to you. On the same block as Josh's record store there'd been a coffee shop where one of the girls who worked there brought her toddler sometimes. The owner told her not to, and whenever she saw his car go past to pull into the parking lot, she'd run out the front door of her shop and into the front door of Josh's and leave her son to sit until her boss left. Josh didn't care because the girl was pretty, and anyway he didn't do shit but plop the little boy in a corner. It was Vera who'd have to play games with him and turn safety hazards into toys, and even though she tried, he always just started screaming, and wouldn't stop until his mother got back. He wouldn't even smile for her. That William was so calm with her seemed like its own argument, like the universe telling her he belonged with her.

One night in November the city was blanketed in unexpected snow. Business operations shut down early. The trains were running slow and cabs were near impossible to flag. Vera wasn't looking forward to the icy walk from the office to the train, or from the train to her apartment. She accepted Derek and Adam's invitation to stay the night. They lived on the upper floor of the loft that housed the office. They put William to bed on the couch, and made her toaster pizza and hot chocolate with shots of rum in it. Though she teased them about their bachelor dinner, it felt good going down. It had been months since she'd spent an evening with people her own age.

Somewhere after their third cup of cocoa, Derek kissed her, or she kissed him, or in any case she spent the night with him, and then the next, and the one after. Within a week she had a toothbrush and a few changes of clothes upstairs in the apartment, and William had a second bed. She saw less and less of the attic in Red Hook, and when she was there she could sometimes see the landlady in the window of the building next door, marking her comings and goings with suspicion.

In December, they threw a holiday party at the loft.

Vera hung garlands and mistletoe and purchased and dec-
orated a small plastic tree. Everyone got drunk on rum-
soaked eggnog and, when that ran out, cheap beer. People
took slightly pornographic pictures making out under the
mistletoe. At a dollar store, Vera had found a box of orna-
ments that were meant to be written on with permanent
marker. She gave one to each of the party guests, and before long the tree was covered in bulbs that said things like
New York I love you but you're bringing me down. William
was passed around from person to person like a particularly lifelike doll, and Vera was feeling charitable enough
to let him be a part of everyone's fantasy of domesticity,
instead of just hers. People had brought him toys and
stuffed animals. Derek bought him a set of wooden blocks.
When he presented a second box, Vera started to protest
that he was spoiling William, but he indicated it was meant
for her. Vera stared for a minute. She'd been counting William's presents as her own and couldn't remember when
she'd stopped seeing herself as a separate entity. She opened
the box Derek had given her, and then put on the glass-
beaded necklace it contained. Derek kissed her.

"I love you," he said.

"You love rum," said Vera.

"I love you and rum," said Derek. He kissed her again.

Later, Vera went into the back room to call her parents.
It was an hour earlier on central time, but still past her
mother's bedtime.

"Why are you waking me up?" her mother asked. "Is everything OK? Why is it so loud?"

"I love you," said Vera.

"Are you drunk?" said her mother. "What are you doing out there?"

"I'm happy," said Vera. "I'm not going to call for a while. I just wanted you to know."

Keeping William made the past firmly the past, the Vera who'd left home a Vera who couldn't exist anymore. She committed to the present. She liked waking up with Derek, the feel of something solid beside her. She liked the way he looked at her and the way he was with William and the way he surprised her. She liked the pattern of her life now, the domestic monotony tempered with the rush of feeling always close to the edge of something, the sensation of having the thing she loved and valuing it all the more because she knew it could all go wrong at any minute.

AND THEN EVERYTHING DID. Jacob, one of the couriers, swerved to miss a puddle and slid into an eighteen-wheeler in Manhattan on a rainy day. Jacob was a nineteen-year-old with startlingly blue eyes, an orthodontically perfect smile, a part-time bartending gig, and an unrealized aspiration to be an actor one day. He had been in Vera's office the day before, picking up a check and giving William a lollipop. He had been at the holiday party a few weeks earlier, drinking flaming tequila shots and kissing a girl with pink highlights and a crescent moon tattooed on the inside of her wrist. There was a somber memorial service, attended by dozens of his friends and fellow couriers, some wearing black bike helmets in solidarity. Vera had bought a black dress and clutched William close to her chest at the service. He had been the only one not crying.

Jacob's mother was a doctor in Connecticut. She hired a law firm. The complaint charged the city with failure to institute proper regulations to ensure the safety of bikers. It charged Brooklyn Delivers with being reckless by expecting unreasonable delivery times and overlooking the myriad ways in which their employees violated safety protocols. All of this was true and—in spite of the unenforceable liability waiver that the employees signed—probably actionable. In the somber aftermath of Jacob's death, Adam and Derek underreacted for the first few weeks. For the better part of a month, they were uncommunicative and high most of the time. Vera stopped spending the night.

At home in her attic apartment Vera stayed up some nights, thinking of Jacob's face the day he'd bent down to give William the lollipop. She thought of his mother's grief, filtered through legalese. One night she imagined the irrevocable loss of William. Even the flicker of pretending he was gone left her with a feeling so complete and unfamiliar that she was wrecked, lay there sobbing so loudly that

William woke up and cried too. She couldn't bring herself to get up and go to him.

At the office, she searched for the first time in months for evidence that whoever had lost him wanted to find him. She clicked half-heartedly through pages of missing-child announcements, neither wanting nor expecting to find William's face. There was photo after photo. A gap-toothed blond boy on his mother's lap. A cocoa-colored girl with beaded braids, grinning and clutching a teddy bear. A seven-year-old with a pink bike. Some of them, Vera knew from the news, had already been found dead. For the others, she imagined improbable scenarios, scenarios in which people like her had rescued them and taken them off to some other life.

On the third page of results, she found a bulletin board for parents of missing children, and under the headline MY SON WILLIAM—MISSING SINCE OCTOBER, Vera finally saw the picture she'd been terrified of seeing: William, the way he'd looked when she found him, his eyes unmistakable. She tried to reason that she'd had her William since August, and so this must be another child, but she read on anyway, sick to her stomach. At the top of the page was his date of birth. He'd be three in April. The man posting the picture said he was William's father. There was a second picture, of him with William and William's mother, the same wispy blond woman from what felt like so long ago. It didn't explain why she wasn't the one looking for him.

It didn't explain how William had gotten from Chicago, where his father lived, to a bus on the Jersey Turnpike. In the second picture, William was an infant. Both the man and the woman were smiling broadly, their eyes sparkling. At the bottom of the post, the man claiming to be William's father had listed the numbers for the police tip line and his own cell phone.

Vera dialed the second number.

"Hello," she said. "May I speak to William Charles Sr.?"

"Speaking," said a steely voice on the other end.

"I'm a reporter," said Vera. "I came across your post about your son. I wondered if I could talk to you about his case?"

"You in New York?" asked the voice. "Your number came up New York."

"Yes. We're a small paper, but we cover national news sometimes if it's of interest. I'm doing a series on missing children."

"I can barely get the Chicago cops to pay attention, let alone the papers," said the man.

"I'm listening," said Vera.

"He was supposed to be with his mother and next thing I know she stops letting me talk to him on the phone. She moved to Jersey, to be with some guy, and said she didn't want me calling. Sometimes I'd call anyway, and get the little girl—not mine, but I'd been around since she was little—and when I'd ask her about William she'd start crying. Then the guy they were living with took off, and my ex turned up dead. Overdose. Poor kid found her mother like that. They gave her to her grandma, who never liked me any, and she either can't or won't say what happened to my boy. All she says is that he wasn't in the house. But he's two. How far could he go?"

"I'm sorry, sir," said Vera.

"I just want my son."

FOR THE NEXT WEEK it was Vera who walked around in a fog. Derek and Adam had gone into panic mode. They'd been cooperating while stalling when they could, but Jacob's mother wouldn't accept a settlement offer until their financial records had been released in discovery. They were worried that a thorough audit would reveal too many irregularities. On Monday Derek asked Vera to stay late. When they locked up for the day, he led her into the back room.

"We're taking off," he said. "New IDs, enough money to lie low for a while. Eventually we'll figure something out. There's a guy with a grow op who thinks everything will be legal soon."

"Where?" said Vera. "When?"

"Cali," said Derek. "Two weeks. Adam knows a guy."

"What am I supposed to do?"

"You can come with us," said Derek. "You should probably get out of town for a while anyway."

The possibility dangled in front of her like a brass ring. She'd come this far. She could go farther. She could keep William. She could keep Derek. She pictured William all grown up, the chubbiness stretched out of his cheeks. "I grew up on a farm," he'd say. "I'm pretty sure my parents did something shady for money, but man were they in love." She tried to picture California but found she didn't even have an image of it in her mind, only a vague fear of earthquakes.

"Get me the paperwork," said Vera. "Let me think about it."

She packed what would fit in her suitcase, and sold the rest. When William's bed was gone she kept him with her, on a blanket on the floor, clinging to him. She gave notice to her landlady and came home from work the next day to find the apartment already being shown to a daunted would-be subletter. At the end of the week, Derek left an envelope on her desk, with a California ID with her picture and the name Jessica. There was also a birth certificate for William, who'd been renamed Joshua. At the office, their days were measured in shredded paper, the whir of the shredding machines a threat and a promise. If everything could be erased, anything could disappear. If you could erase everything, you could start again.

SHE WANTED TO SEE the father before she made any decisions. She equivocated on making Derek any promises. She didn't love him enough to make up for William's potential absence, and so she didn't see the point in pretending. She helped him pack. She kept his necklace around her neck. She buzzed Derek's locks off with an electric razor. She dyed Adam's blond hair black. Vera spent Derek and Adam's last night in New York at the loft with them. She made margaritas. She curled up in Derek's arms and imagined trying to explain to him how much bigger her guilt was than theirs. She got up before dawn and made them breakfast and kissed Derek goodbye. He offered to leave her with an address of a person he said would be able to tell her where to find them, and she said maybe it was better if he didn't.

The next day, she and William got on a bus to Chicago. She bundled him in layers of winter clothing—a turtleneck, a sweater, a hooded jacket, and the hat Derek had bought him. He was uncharacteristically fussy, insisting that he was hot and itchy. One by one the outer layers were removed. From their stopover in Cleveland, Vera called Eileen, a friend in school in Chicago. She hadn't seen Eileen in years, but they'd gone to high school together, and when she said she needed a place to stay for the night, Eileen offered to come get her at the bus station.

"My God, you have a kid!" she said when she saw them. "He's so big."

"He's almost three," said Vera.

"How was New York?" asked Eileen.

"Beautiful," said Vera. "Exhausting."

Eileen brought them back to her one-bedroom apartment in Hyde Park. She pulled out the sofa and told Vera to make herself at home. Vera turned on a cartoon show and combed William's hair. She kissed the top of his head and told him she loved him. She remembered being a child, seated between her mother's legs watching TV while her mother parted and braided her hair, and felt, for the first time in years, homesick, sick for everything she could still lose.

She slept poorly. Over coffee, Vera asked if Eileen could keep an eye on William while she ran a quick errand. Vera took a cab to William's father's address. It was an old brick row house, beaten up a bit, but not neglected. The lawn was mowed, and the shutters had been recently painted. She walked around the block a few times and feigned interest in a house for sale across the street. BANK OWNED! read its sign. On her fifth circle around the block, she saw the door to the house open, and the man from the photograph come out, then turn behind him to help an older woman down the stairs. Both of them resembled William. He had a father. He had a grandmother. He had never been hers. They looked up. For a second, Vera thought William

Sr. was pointing at her, and she was ready to confess. Then she realized he was pointing past her, at the foreclosed house, its overgrown lawn.

BACK AT EILEEN'S, Vera found William circling the living room, clutching a teddy bear while Eileen typed a paper. Vera made grilled cheese for lunch. She told Eileen that she and William had another bus to catch, all the way to California, and would be gone that evening. In the afternoon, Eileen left for class, and told Vera to lock the door behind her on the way out. Vera hugged her goodbye. Eileen ruffled William's hair.

"Lucky boy you are," she said. "Such a big trip, for such a little person."

The moment Eileen was out the door, Vera set fire to William's forged birth certificate with a cigarette lighter, afraid she'd be unable to resist the temptation to keep him otherwise. She started a letter three times. On the first attempt, she emphasized that she hadn't meant to take him, that it felt like he'd been given to her and she just hadn't questioned it. A paragraph in, she realized this wasn't her story anymore, that the point was not her own defense. In the second version, she focused on all of William's milestones: her favorite things about him, his best days—she wanted to show he'd been happy and unharmed, but when she reread the letter it seemed cruel, to emphasize the time his father had missed and wouldn't get back. In her third and final effort, she tried to account in a matter-of-fact way for the time she'd kept him, to assure his father that she'd done her best not to damage him, that he had not fallen into terrible hands, that he had suffered no irreparable trauma, that she was not a person who would ever harm him, though of course she understood now that she had. She held William in her arms until he fell asleep, then picked him up and tucked him into Eileen's bed. She texted to confirm Eileen was on her way home. She left the note for William's father and the note she'd written for Eileen, with William's father's name and address, sitting on the coffee table, next to Eileen's apartment key. She walked three blocks and hailed a cab.

On the way to the bus station, the city went by in a blur of brick and beige and gray. Vera was startled and shaking. Adam and Derek were waiting until they could be found again, but Vera understood now that she would need to be lost forever, would need to let the whole of the murky country swallow her up. The cabdriver thought she was drunk and kept offering to pull over if she needed to throw up. The third time he offered, she said yes, but when she opened the door and leaned out, nothing came up. There was just the shock of the cold, and the dry empty heave of her belly.

The Office of
Historical Corrections

Our office was tucked away in a back corridor of one of the city's labyrinth brutalist buildings, all beige concrete and rows of square windows. I had never minded DC's lingering architecture; I had been in college before I understood I was meant to find it ugly and not cozily utilitarian. But I had grown up with the architecture, grown up idealizing people who worked in buildings like mine, and besides, I liked to remember that the term *brutalism* came not from any aesthetic assessment, but from the French for "raw concrete." Since starting at the institute, I had formally corrected mistaken claims about the term's etymology seven times. Small corrections usually made me feel pitiful and pedantic, but I liked making that one, liked to think of us, not just the people in my office, but all of the city's remaining civil servants, as people trying to make something solid out of what raw material we had been given, liked to think that we were in the right setting to do our jobs.

Of course, as a field agent, I rarely spent a full day indoors. Often that freedom felt like a luxury, but it was June—not quite the worst of summer, but hot enough that walking my regular daily rounds left me flecked with sweat and constantly looking for excuses to go indoors. Some days I went into shops full of kitsch and corrected souvenirs with their dates wrong just to absorb the air-conditioning. After everything else, I would remember how often I had been bored at the beginning of that summer, how worried I was that our work had become inconsequential, how I had wondered whether I would ever again be a part of anything that mattered.

The vision for the Institute for Public History that summoned me from my former job as a history professor at GW had been grandiose. An ambitious freshman congresswoman demanded funding to put a public historian in every zip code in the country, a correction for what she called the contemporary crisis of truth. It was pitched as a new public works project for the intellectual class, so many of us lately busy driving cars and delivering groceries and completing tasks on demand to make ends meet. Government jobs would put all those degrees to work and be comparatively lucrative. The congresswoman envisioned a national network of fact-checkers and historians, a friendly citizen army devoted to making the truth so accessible and appealing it could not be ignored. We had started as a research institute, loosely under the direction of the Library of Congress—an NIH for a different sort of public health crisis. We were the solution for decades of bad information and bad faith use of it. Our work was to protect the historical record, not to pick fights (guideline 1) or correct people's readings of current news (guideline 2).

The post-election energy that created us had stalled almost immediately; the former congresswoman was now a TV pundit. At the institute, we were only forty people total, twenty of us headquartered in DC. The reduced parameters of our mission often led people to assume we were overzealous tour guides or long-winded museum employees who had strayed from our home base. Some of my colleagues leaned into the misunderstanding: Bill circled monuments correcting tourists with their facts mixed up, sometimes just by reading them the placards they'd walked by; Sophie rarely worked beyond the Smithsonian grounds; Ed hung out in breweries all day, but he checked in each week with such a lengthy log of plausible corrections no one was sure whether he was a friendly and efficient drunk or a gifted writer of fictional dialogue.

I had been at IPH for four years then, and I wanted to take my charge seriously. To keep from falling into routine, I assigned myself a different DC neighborhood each month. For June, I was in Capitol Hill, where shortly after correcting a tourist who thought the Rayburn Building was named after Gene Rayburn, I realized it was lunchtime. The block surrounding me was cluttered with restaurants that had puns for names and sold expensive comfort food from ostentatiously nostalgic chrome countertops; it all felt sinister and I had settled on pizza when I walked past a bakery, its pink awning reading CAKE EVERYDAY COUNT in loopy cursive that mimicked frosting. I hated the name—the attempt at a double entendre failing to properly be even a single entendre—but it was Daniel's birthday, and I caught the towering cupcake trees in the window display, heaps of red and cocoa and gold. Cupcakes would seem light and full of options, I thought, and so I walked in and considered flavors before deciding cupcakes were wrong, a variety of cupcakes would say I was a child who could not make up her mind, or else invite him to imagine the opposite—me fully domesticated and walking triumphantly into a PTA meeting, as if that were the future I was waiting for him to offer me. I walked farther down the counter, past the wedding cakes, and the photorealistic DC landmark cakes, and the cakes carved into shoes and champagne bottles and cartoons, looking for something unobtrusive.

The correction was so minor that four-years-ago-me would have decided it wasn't worth it. A display cake read JUNETEENTH! in red frosting, surrounded by red, white, and blue stars and fireworks. A flyer taped to the counter

above it encouraged patrons to consider ordering a Juneteenth cake early: *We all know about the Fourth of July!* the
flyer said. *But why not start celebrating freedom a few weeks
early and observe the anniversary of the Emancipation Proclamation! Say it with cake!* One of the two young women
behind the bakery counter was Black, but I could guess the
bakery's owner wasn't. The neighborhood, the prices, the
twee acoustic music drifting out of sleek speakers: I knew
all of the song's words, but everything about the space said
who it was for. My memories of celebrating Juneteenth
in DC were my parents taking me to someone's backyard
BBQ, eating banana pudding and peach cobbler and straw-
berry cake made with Jell-O mix; at not one of them had I
seen a seventy-five-dollar bakery cake that could be carved
into the shape of a designer handbag for an additional fee.
The flyer's sales pitch—so much hanging on that *We all
know*—was targeted not to the people who'd celebrated
Juneteenth all along but to office managers who'd feel hec-
tored into not missing a Black holiday or who just wanted
an excuse for miscellaneous dessert.

"Excuse me," I said, my finger still resting on the coun-
tertop above the flyer. The young Black woman turned
around.

"You want that cake?" she asked.

"No," I said. "Hi. I'm Cassie. I'm with the Institute for
Public History."

The white woman turned around, but both women

looked at me without registering that the name meant anything.

"It's not a big deal," I said. "We don't give orders or anything. We're a public service. Like 311! But I thought you'd
like to know that this flyer's not quite correct. The Emancipation Proclamation was issued in September 1862. Juneteenth is celebrated nationally because it's become a holiday
for the whole diaspora, but it actually recognizes the date
slaves in Texas learned they were free, which was in June
1865, after the end of the Civil War."

"Mmkay," said the white woman.

"I'm just going to leave a note. A tiny correction."

I pulled out a corrections sticker—double holographed
and printed, at considerable expense, with a raised seal;
though easily mocked they were almost never properly
duplicated. I typed the correction into the office's one fu-
turistic indulgence—the handheld printers we'd all been
issued when we were first hired—and ran a sticker through
it to print my text. I signed my name and the date, peeled
it from its backing, and affixed it to the counter beside the
flyer.

"There," I said. "No biggie."

I smiled and met both women's eyes. We were not supposed to be aggressive in demanding people's time—correct
the misinformation as swiftly and politely as possible (guideline 3)—but we were supposed to make it clear we were available for further inquiry or a longer conversation if anyone

wanted to know more (guideline 5). We were supposed to be prepared to cite our sources (guideline 7).

"You gonna buy a cake?" said the Black woman. "Or you came in about the flyer?"

"Oh," I said. "Yes. I'm kind of dating someone and it's his birthday. I was trying to decide what kind of cake would be best. Or I don't know, maybe cupcakes are better. Do you have any favorites?"

"Ma'am, if you show up for your man's birthday with you and a cake and he complains about it, you're not even kind of dating him anymore. It doesn't matter the kind of cake."

"You're right," I said. "Give me that one."

I pointed at something labeled BLACKOUT CAKE. "Like an Oreo cookie without the cream" said the description. I could tell Daniel I had bought him the blackest cake in the store. The boxes were pink with whimsical phrases written in gold; I asked for the one with CAKE FOR DAYS on it. I would let him decide whether to make the dirty joke, or complain about the cultural appropriation of white-owned businesses, or go with the obvious Oreo commentary. I would leave out the bit about my correction. Daniel was a journalist, skeptical by both nature and training, and he found my work suspicious at best.

He wasn't alone. Before I'd left GW for the institute, I had been on an upward trajectory, had been lucky. I could recite the academia warning speech I had been given and was supposed to give promising students in return: you had to be willing to go anywhere, to leave anyone, to work for any paltry amount if you wanted to work in your field, and even then, there was probably no job, or no chance that out of a hundred PhDs who applied, you'd be the one to get it. But I had done just one year of a four-four visiting gig in the Midwest before landing a well-regarded tenure track job, a two-two job not just in a major city but in the city I was from. The DC of my childhood was gone, of course, whole swaths the city felt familiar now only because I remembered less of what they used to be, but it was still the only place I'd ever felt at home. Landing a good academic job here was serendipity bordering on magic in a market where "professor" increasingly meant teaching seven classes on four different campuses for no health insurance and below minimum wage.

I missed my students and colleagues after leaving, missed working on the manuscript that no one asked me about anymore—my years of research on Odetta Holmes still in file drawers. I missed the particular playacted pretension and permanent adolescence that characterized academic parties, and, I admit, I missed the ways that being near the top of a crumbling enterprise had still felt like the top. But, when the chance to work at IPH came, I'd left all of that to do what felt more immediately meaningful.

My parents had relished introducing me as Dr. Jacobs, the history professor, and now didn't quite know what to say I was. I had tried to explain to them that *professor*, even in its best incarnation, now meant answering every year to the tyranny of metrics and enrollments, meant spinning what you loved because you loved it and valued because it was valuable into a language of corporate speak to convince administrators your students were employable. It meant being told you were the problem if you coddled students too much, you, the last chance to prepare them for the sink-or-swim world, but also you were the problem if the students were in crisis, if you didn't warn someone in time that a student was a danger to themselves, if you didn't have a plan for how to keep your classroom in the fifty-year-old building with doors that didn't lock anymore safe if a student with a gun showed up. It meant being told each year in a celebratory fashion that the faculty was now more diverse than ever, and then, at some more somber meeting a few months later, being given a list of all the acts of self-governance faculty would no longer be trusted to do and all the evaluative metrics that would now be considered more strictly. It meant being given well-intentioned useless advice from senior colleagues who floated in denial that the institutions they'd devoted their lives to were over as they had known them, but reminded by your more precarious colleagues that you had it too good to complain.

It had been hard for me to convince people—even the people at IPH itself, who had been mostly recruiting from the surplus of PhDs without full-time jobs—that I had really wanted to leave. The best I could explain it was that I loved my work and hated watching it disappear.

THE INSTITUTE was not without its detractors. The proposal alone had incited a chorus of libertarian panic. In our first year, there were seventeen different social media accounts devoted just to monitoring our corrections; the accounts called us, depending on their angle of critique, The Big Brother Institute, or The Department of Political Correctness, or The Bureau of Whitewashing, or, once in a major paper's op-ed, The Office of Historical Corrections, which was intended to be dismissive but felt enough like our actual mission that it had become a running office joke, the imaginary shadow entity on which we blamed all missteps and bad publicity. *The Office of Historical Corrections strikes again!*

The attention economy was our nemesis and our cheapest tool. About half of the historians worked primarily online. Originally, each had a friendly profile with their name and picture and credentials, meant to make them accessible and unintimidating, but all three of the women of color complained that every time they made a correction their replies flooded with personal vitriol. They tried randomizing log-ins, so that each day's corrections were not necessarily linked to the agent who'd issued them, which pleased no one: white men did not like being called ugly cunts any better than anyone else, it turned out, and the women of color who had complained in the first place did not like feeling uncredited for their labor, or appreciate the erasure of the professional voices they had cultivated. Everyone with a desk job now worked from a shared faceless account, which did, admittedly, look somewhat ominous and bureaucratic, but was generally cheerful in tone.

We did the best we could. There was an agent primarily devoted to sending strongly worded letters to the publishers of inaccurate textbooks, but we did not go to schools and classrooms (guideline 4). Our purpose was limited to correction of the historical record, which our mission defined as events at least one year old (guideline 2, part b). We were to make every effort to avoid or back away from the kind of confrontation likely to escalate to force or police intervention (guideline 1). We were supposed to avoid meaningless and pedantic corrections (guideline 8), but the work attracted the pedantic. We had done a month of damage control after one of my more zealous colleagues publicly embarrassed a popular influencer over her pronunciation of "Ulysses" in a fashion vlog she'd posted from Grant's Tomb. The influencer dubbed us The Office of Mansplaining, which was picked up by at least a thousand of her million followers. I was one of three women of color who were field historians with the project at the time; in the wake of the controversy, I had been sent by the director to be profiled in *The Post*, to show we were inclusive and nonthreatening.

The most persistent of our resistance came from the Free Americans, a group of white supremacists who preferred to be called white preservationists. Their leader had turned forty last year but was frequently described by the press as having boyish charm. He was soft-spoken and had a doctorate in psychology. He claimed to hate both violence and the spotlight, but he frequently appeared on television and at marches that turned into brawls. A few years earlier he'd been on the cover of a national magazine in a tailored suit and ascot, which had become such a joke that all members now wore ascots, though many continued to mark themselves by getting the same tattoo: an elk's head with FREE MEN FREE FISTS NO FREE LUNCHES written between the antlers. Violence seemed to turn up where they did, but officially they were deemed responsible for only three deaths: an anarchist kid beaten after dueling protests, a Salvadoran man heckled and stabbed on his way home from work by a rowdy chapter leaving a bar, and a white college student shot and dumped into a lake after she argued with her boyfriend about his affiliation with the group. They had never physically attacked an IPH agent, though the Oakland field agent quit after an upsetting run-in. They staged protests against us, following a field historian around for the day, or papering over all of the corrections stickers in a given city with their own revisions, but they were more interested in the publicity than in us specifically, we'd realized, and when the press around us was quieter, mostly so were they.

I MADE ONLY THREE CORRECTIONS after the bakery, and then I circled the reflecting pool several times without hearing anything more incorrect than celebrity gossip and unscientific speculation about the mating habits of ducks. I suspected that under its ornamental and slightly profane box, my cake was melting, so I decided to bring it safely to the office refrigerator and use the rest of the afternoon to type up reports. In the lobby, I flashed my badge at the security guard and took the elevator to the seventh floor, where we had been shoved into an open office space that a different government agency had argued its way out of based on studies showing reduced efficiency.

I didn't mind the close quarters; I wasn't confined to my desk most of the time, and when I was there Elena was on the other side of it. We had started together at the beginning of the enterprise and bonded quickly: Elena worked online and I worked in the field; Elena was a Chicana from LA and I was a Black girl from DC; Elena had a husband and three kids and I had what Elena charitably called a free spirit, but we shared an urgency about the kind of work we were doing, a belief that the truth was our last best hope, and a sense that our own mission was less neutral and more necessary than that of the white men we answered to at the office.

"What's the cake for?" Elena asked.

"Daniel's birthday," I said.

"Hmm," said Elena.

"What?"

"I guess it's your turn to make the effort."

"It's not about effort. That's the whole point of not really dating. It's easy. No one has to make the effort."

"Hold on, I'm writing down the date."

"Why?"

"Because I can't correct you until a year from now. Guideline 2."

"See, I almost brought you a cupcake, but then I remembered you're mean."

"You really didn't bring me a cupcake?"

"I actually was going to, but I had to make a correction in the bakery, and I got flustered and forgot. Plus the girl who worked there already thought I was crazy."

"You corrected a cake?"

"I corrected a flyer in a cake shop."

"Well, boss wants to see you. He left a note." Elena pointed to my desk. "Maybe don't lead with the cake bit."

I read the note, but it was inscrutable. I could not recall being involved in anything controversial lately—my recent corrections had been rather uniformly underwhelming—but our supervision was so generally lax that I felt like I'd been called to the principal's office. The director had been running a prestigious university's ethnomusicology institute before he'd been invited to steer the organization. While he managed most days to look the DC part in suits and close-cropped hair, and he kept all the institute's moving pieces more or less moving, he had the energy of a man who had intended to spend his golden years playing guitar on the beach and was daily bewildered by what had gone wrong.

"Cassie," he said when I walked into his office. "We have a Genevieve problem. It might take some legwork to sort out."

He tapped a folder on his desk. A clarification request. The requests that made it past initial review were mostly cases where the historian's initial correction had been over-zealous, frequently violations of guideline 6: we do not posit certainty where the facts are actually murky or disputed, or intervene in a dispute over something so trivial that the relevant information cannot be verified except by weighing the accounts of the disputing parties. Presently, though, the institute was working its way through a backlog of clarification requests all triggered by the recently departed Genevieve Marchand.

Genevieve had been gone from IPH for six months, but she had been regularly reappearing as my nemesis for most of my life. We first met in the fourth grade, when Genevieve was still Genie and had, until the moment of our introduction, been the only Black girl in her class at the private school where I landed a scholarship. Our parents moved, broadly, in the same Black professional circles, but my father was a lawyer who had started with the Bureau of Consumer Protection and then moved into the sort of lawyering that advertised on the radio stations that were banned in Genie's home (*No Money? No Problems! At 1-800-TROUBLE your lawyer gets paid when you do*); Genie's mother was a sitting judge. My mother had recently moved from civil rights work in the Department of Justice to civil rights work in the Department of Education; Genie's father owned part of a tech company and had his name on a wing of our school. My parents were first-generation upper middle class, and Genie's were nearly as old money as Black money got to be in the U.S., which is to say, not terribly old but extremely proud of it.

My parents and I were invited over to their house after my first week of school. In the middle of the dessert course, Genie's father said, "She's so well spoken, for having been in public school until now," and my mother grimaced and launched into a defense of public schools, and my father politely waited for her to finish and then said, "When your baby's really brilliant you don't need to pay for someone to tell you so. You wait for the opportunities to come to you." Genie's father hinted that my scholarship was possible because of funds they'd earmarked for the recruitment of minority students, and my mother said true charity wasn't boastful, and Genie's mother noted that the Bible verse my mother was trying to quote was actually about love. That was how joint family dinners went for the following decade, but they continued to happen several times a year.

At the dinner table, Genie was a proper young lady and I was a mouthy child being raised in a home where I'd never been told *Children should be seen and not* heard, or *Stay out of grown folks'* business. Beyond our parents' watch, Genie had plenty to say. She did not so much actively dislike me as disdain me. Her favorite thing to do was pronounce something I was doing, or wearing, or simply was, to be confusing. "Your hair is confusing me," Genie said the first day we met, with an air of genuine concern that never entirely went away or became less grating. In both our households there were a series of party pictures of the two of us, one per party each year from childhood to adolescence. I liked myself just fine when looking at myself, but in photos with Genie, a former Gerber baby, belle of the Jack and Jill debutante ball, I looked sulky, ersatz. It was too late for the era when prestigious institutions would acquire one minority and stop, but too soon for there to be enough of us that we had the option of avoiding taking a position on each other. We grew up circling each other, each aware of the ways the other highlighted our deficiencies.

I went to college expecting to be mostly rid of Genie. For the four years we spent at well-regarded universities on opposite coasts, I became accustomed to her absence, but at the party Genie's parents threw for her graduation, we discovered we were both headed directly to the same PhD program. Ready to believe in the comfort of the familiar, we tried that first year to be real friends, went on study dates and girls' nights and salon outings, built the trappings of a closeness that never quite took. We were the only two Black women in the department—this counting faculty, grad students, staff, and, for four out of our five years, undergraduate majors—and in our first year I was constantly correcting people who got the two of us confused, our similar hair and coloring enough to override that Genie was five inches taller and three dress sizes smaller than I was. The confusion eventually faded because professors in the program liked me fine, but they loved Genie, and in that way they came to be able to tell the difference between us. Our pretense at true friendship also faded. In my telling, Genie discovered she didn't need it, and in Genie's telling, I discovered I didn't want it. It was true, I admit—away from Genie, I had the peculiar confidence of only children, the boldness that came from being doted on but alone often enough to be oblivious to my own strangeness. In Genie's presence, I felt revealed by the only nearby witness to my life as a whole.

At the end of our first year in the program, I visited my parents, who were in the suburbs now—they had given up on DC rent and moved to PG county—and told them there wasn't anyone to date seriously in my small white university town. A week later we drove into DC for Genie's parents' annual summer white party, where Genie announced her engagement to James Harmon III, a Black doctor who'd just finished his residency there. Genie got married the summer after our second year, just before her husband started work at the University Hospital. I was invited, but I was teaching a summer class and couldn't cancel sessions; I sent, via my parents, my apologies and a Vitamix. My research area was protest movements of the twentieth century, and Genie's was material culture in the seventeenth century, which meant although we were both Americanists, after our first year of school we generally shared only one class a semester, and saw less and less of each other.

By our third year, Genie and her husband had moved into a spectacular town house, at which she volunteered to host the annual grad student end-of-year party. In previous years, the party had consisted of chips and beer in an overheated basement apartment, or supermarket cheese plates in the student union room, but Genie's party was catered, except for the gingerbread Bundt cake she baked and iced herself, using her grandmother's recipe. Professional bartenders in black tie were on hand serving cocktails named after schools of historical thought. Genie drank only The Great Man, which was actually a mocktail, and confided in me that she was pregnant. I congratulated her, genuinely, and felt resentful that I could not allow myself even a moment of smug anti-feminist joy to think that motherhood might slow Genie down or at least keep her off the job market when it was my turn. At least I am having a twenties, I thought, though my twenties, which I'd treated with a cast-down-your-bucket-where-you-are approach, had thus far only brought me a string of men who were all very sad about some quality in themselves that they had no intention of making any effort to change. I took a sip of my Marxist, a vodka cocktail made with such high-end alcohol that at first sip I hadn't recognized it as vodka, having until that party believed that it was the essence of vodka to have an aftertaste like astringent.

Genie went straight from grad school to a fabulous job the same year I headed off for my visiting position; when I landed the tenure-track job a year later, she sent a note of congratulations written on stationery from her own higher-ranked university. For years I had only peripheral knowledge of her life—talks and publications, family photos shared on social media. She and James had a daughter, Octavia, who appeared to take to the camera the way Genie had as a child, and I watched her grow from baby-faced to long-limbed and theatrical. There'd been no note of congratulations when I joined IPH, and when Genie and her family stopped appearing in my social media feeds I thought maybe I'd been downsized from her Friends roster, having become professionally unimportant. When she reappeared, to my astonishment, it was to join IPH two years after I had. She was divorced, parted from her tenure-track job in her pre-tenure year under murky circumstances rumored to involve a lawsuit, had shaved her hair down to a crisp teenie Afro, and no longer went by Genie—it was Genevieve now.

The Genie I remembered would have had expansive ideas about our mission but would have spent years charming the director into coming around to them, while parroting her parents on the virtues of treading lightly. *Genevieve* said in our first office meeting during her first week that we were tiptoeing around history to the point that we might as well be lying to people. She wanted a guideline emphasizing that lies of omission were still lies. In the field, she amended a sign quoting the Declaration of Independence with portions of the worst of *Notes on the State of Virginia*. She was instructed not to come back to the National Portrait Gallery after she stood in front of the Gauguin for hours telling viewers about his abuse of underage Tahitian girls. She made a tourist child cry at Mount Vernon when she talked about Washington's vicious pursuit of his runaway slaves, and she was formally asked by the only Virginia field historian to avoid making further corrections in the state. The following month she talked her way into the Kennedy Center and "corrected" hundreds of programs for that evening's showing of a beloved musical where George Washington was written as a kindly paternal figure, noting that in real life Washington had not been a jovial singing Black man, and including an extensive list of his atrocities. She was, she protested when our director reprimanded her, not in the state of Virginia when she made the correction.

That was the only Genevieve clarification I had previously been called in for—less a clarification really, and more a minor PR campaign. I got complimentary tickets to the show and brought Daniel. A picture of us in the audience ran on the agency account, along with an apologia for having overstepped. *We know the difference between history and artistry*, the post said. I didn't write it—I didn't work online—and Elena had refused the assignment; the actual text was written by one of the two white men named Steve whom I couldn't always tell apart because I'd never learned their last names. IPH hadn't needed me to weigh in; they'd only needed my face, to show that I was one of the reasonable ones. My face only barely held up its part of the bargain—in the picture, Daniel looked quizzical and I was grimacing. I had never seen the show before and was inclined to agree with Genevieve's critique, if not her methods.

I didn't say any of that to the director, but I took Genevieve out for a drink at an upscale Black-owned bar on U Street to apologize. We had socialized minimally since she'd started at the agency, and though we blamed it on working mostly outside of the office, and Genevieve juggling joint custody, I knew it wasn't scheduling that stood between us. I was sincere enough in being sorry for my role in things that we left the bar almost on good terms, but on our way back to Metro, we passed a bar with a young and multiracial crowd and a weekly hip-hop and classic rock dance party. Its name—Dodge City—was a nod to both its country-western decor and DC's derogatory nickname from the '90s, when the city was the country's murder capital and so many people, most of them young and Black, were killed in its streets that a joke about the likelihood of being shot there became a way of saying where you were from.

Genevieve wanted to go inside and footnote the bar's name on the cocktail menus with an explanation of the violence it referenced, and I had to threaten to call the director before she relented. I walked home, furious at still being the bad guy, and also remembering the way Genevieve's parents had talked about the revival of U Street when we were children, the way Genevieve had adopted their disdain in adolescence, how much they'd spoken of the city's past and future, and how little they'd wanted to be connected with the Black people living in its dilapidated present until most of them had been pushed out. Where was the correction for that?

Genevieve gave up on me again. For her remaining time at IPH, our interactions stopped at cordial acknowledgment. It was the kind of tension that in the beginning seemed it might still be resolved, but went on long enough that the grievance settled, turned so solid that trying to make pleasant chitchat around it would have felt disrespectful. Besides, I knew if I did resolve things with her, I would end up in the middle of whatever battle she picked next, and I couldn't afford that. I told myself that in the institute's good graces, I could still do some good.

If it had only been the occasional play or bar that Genevieve raised a fuss about, she might have lasted longer, but Genevieve's most persistent and controversial grievance was the passive voice atrocity: wherever there was a memorial, she wanted to name not just the dead but the killers. She corrected every memorial to lynching, every note about burnt schoolhouses and destroyed business districts, murdered leaders and bombed churches, that failed to say exactly who had done it. She thought the insistence on victims without wrongdoers was at the base of the whole American problem, the lie that supported all the others. She upset people. She jeopardized the whole project, and for nothing, said our more liberal colleagues. She was not correcting falsehoods, said the more conservative, she was adding revisionist addendums. They said these things to my face, assuming, because we did not seem to be friends, that I disagreed with her.

My problem, alas, had never been as simple as Genie being wrong. In fourth grade, she'd been right about my hair: I had insisted on doing it myself, and my parents were willing to let me learn through trial and error. In high school, Genie might have found a nicer way to put it than

"You know they only keep telling you you're a good poet because they expect us to be illiterate?" but my poetry wasn't actually as good as teachers' praise for it. In grad school, Genie asked me once what my parents wanted for me, and I said that they just wanted me to be happy. Genie said "That explains a lot then," and I said "What?" and Genie said "I've met a lot of Black women who had to learn it was OK to choose to be happy, but you're the only one I know who was raised to expect it."

It was hard to reconcile people-pleasing Genie with abrasive Genevieve, but they had in common usually being correct. IPH disagreed and had forced her out after just over a year and a dozen write-ups for policy violations. Being indignant on Genevieve's behalf was unsettling. The very fact of Genie being Genevieve was unsettling. Just as I was accepting that I had grown into as much of a different person as I was ever going to become, Genevieve showed up proving it was still possible to entirely reinvent yourself. Perhaps in whatever years Genie was turning into Genevieve, I was supposed to have been turning into someone called Cassandra. Worse, perhaps I had already turned into Cassandra; perhaps it was Cassandra who made her white colleagues feel so comfortable that they whispered to her while waiting for the coffee to brew or the microwave to ding, "Genevieve—she's a lot, isn't she?" Cassandra whom the director trusted to fix Genevieve's missteps on behalf of the U.S. government. Perhaps I'd been Cassandra for some time now, walking around using some bolder girl's name.

IN THE DIRECTOR'S OFFICE, I opened the blue folder with a suspicion that it would become obvious to me why I had been chosen for this assignment, why this particular Genevieve problem needed a Black woman's face. The issue surrounded a memorial plaque in Cherry Mill, Wisconsin, a small town in the Fox River Valley, about an hour northwest of Milwaukee. Technically, we were federal; Wisconsin was not out of bounds—we could make corrections on vacation, even—but no one from the DC office would be sent there without special circumstances, so what Genevieve had been doing in Wisconsin was for her to know and the clarification file to guess. A generation ago someone would have stopped her from going at all: Cherry Mill had been a sundown town by reputation if not actual ordinance. From the dawn of its existence through the 1980 census it had zero Black residents, officially. In 1937 it apparently had one, briefly, though he was gone before a census caught him: a man named Josiah Wynslow. He'd gone from Mississippi to Chicago and Chicago to Milwaukee. In Milwaukee he'd come into luck—somehow he'd leaped from his job at a meat-packing plant to one as a driver and general errand boy for a Milwaukee tanner who, having watched what the war, the Depression, and the sheer passage of time did to industries and the workers in them, moonlighted as a radical socialist. He died, childless and ornery enough to leave Josiah most of his money. It was less than it would have been before the Depression, much less than it would have been when the tanning industry was in its heyday, but it was still a small fortune for a Black man a decade removed from Mississippi share-cropping.

It was hard to say from the record what his boss meant of the gift—whether it was a gesture of kindness, or a final experiment, or a fuck-you to the society he felt had failed itself—but Josiah took the money, sold his share of the business, and left the city. Even Milwaukee, eventually one of the Blackest cities in the country, barely had a Black population in the '30s, and what there was had been redlined into two diminishing neighborhoods and waxed and waned with the fortunes of the plants that occasionally recruited from Chicago. Josiah, for reasons the file knew not, left Milwaukee for the even whiter and more openly hostile Cherry Mill, where he bought a defunct printing shop from a white man who was about to lose it to the bank, with the apparent intention of turning it into his own tannery and leather goods shop. On the subject of race, Wisconsin was a strange cocktail of progressivism and old-fashioned American anti-Blackness. It had passed one of the earliest civil rights ordinances in the country in 1895 but immediately reduced the remedy for discrimination so much that it wasn't worth the cost of court to sue. Portions of the state had been welcoming enough, if pushed by protest, in its early history, but as in many northern cities, as the number of Black residents grew, so did the number of restrictions on where they could live, socialize, be served, or own property. There had never been a lynching in the state of Wisconsin, the heyday of the Klan was over, and Wisconsin had stayed so white for so long that for decades its local Klan mostly harassed Italians, but no place remained unwelcoming through innocence. There were no restrictive covenants in Cherry Mill when Josiah arrived because previously there had been no one in town to restrict. The man who sold him the location took the money and ran before he had to answer to his neighbors, but find out the neighbors did, and Josiah was repeatedly told to leave town and leave the deed behind or have it taken by force. Repeatedly he did not go.

Josiah was thirty in 1937, old enough to remember the South before he'd left it and the Midwest when he'd arrived, Tulsa and Chicago in 1919, and St. Louis before that, still raw in communal memory. He should have known better than to stay put, and still he stayed put, stayed for months, until a group of concerned citizens came in the night and set the place on fire. He had not finished clearing out the old printing debris and had already hauled in some of his tanning supplies; the basement was stocked with barrels of lye and the place was completely engulfed before he had a chance to get out. For years, this had been openly bragged about, a warning to anyone who might try it next. By the '60s it had become a quiet open secret, and then a nearly lost memory, until it was rediscovered by a graduate student in the late '90s doing archive work with the local newspaper. The result of the ensuing town meetings and public shame was a memorial plaque that went up at the former site of the building where Josiah died.

The sign was there for decades, long enough that it went generally unnoticed. Then Genevieve spotted it. She issued a correction and took the additional liberty of not just stickering but replacing the existing plaque: hers added to Josiah's name the names of those known to have partici-pated in the mob, names known because they had identi-fied themselves in a surviving photograph of the spectacle. Eight of Cherry Mill's adults, seven men, two with small children sitting on their shoulders, and one woman, smiling and holding an infant, had posed and smiled for a photo-graph that someone had captioned *The Cherry Mill Defend-ers: Fire Purifies.* Their names and the date were on the back, in neat cursive penmanship. This, I gathered, was what had set Genevieve digging, what had made her upset enough to go looking for the sign to amend it.

"Let me guess," I said to the director, once I had scanned the file. "Someone is sure there's been an error and their dear grandfather who wouldn't have hurt a fly wasn't a part of this ugliness. It was his doppelgänger in the photo and his name on the sign is a mistake and they want it taken down."

"Not quite. A guy—one Andy Detry—did go looking because his grandfather was named, but he says his grand-father was a right bastard and he was looking to see what became of the victim's family afterward, and whether there was anything he could do to help set things right. What he found, he says, was the victim might not have been killed. Says his digging turned up two death certificates and some living relatives to suggest the victim escaped very much alive and went back to Illinois, where he went on to have a big family. Josiah's surviving relatives joined the clarification request."

"Can't we just correct it then?" I asked.

"Well there's a problem," he said.

"We need to know whose body they claimed was Josiah's?"

"Not exactly. There's no record that there was a body. Total structural collapse and a town full of people who were eager to reclaim the land. Under those circumstances I imagine the word of witnesses would be enough for a death certificate and probably some shenanigans about the deed or the next of kin—after he died, the property somehow turned up in the name of the husband of the woman in the picture. But I'm not asking you to solve an eighty-year-old hypothetical property crime. The body I'm worried about is very much alive. Genevieve has been emailing the office and threatening FOIA requests on this one if we don't keep her updated. I wouldn't be surprised if she's still asking questions of the people of Cherry Mill too. Her sign kicked up some fuss there, and there could be media on this one."

"You're sending me so if there's news footage of an agent taking down a memorial sign with Genevieve screaming in the background, it's two Black women yelling at each other and not a white guy in a suit tearing down the evidence of a crime?"

"I'm sending you because you have good sense and you're not looking for the attention. You can wear a suit if you'd like. Whether or not we list the killers is a philosophical question that I know we don't all see the same way. Whether someone forged a will or a deed or a death certificate to acquire the property is out of our jurisdiction entirely. But whether they declared a living man dead and we doubled down on their mistake—that's facts. And if you find it to be true that the sign is a mistake, Genevieve will take it better coming from you than from anyone else in this office."

"Genevieve will or the *Post* will?"

"It is very much my hope that this clarification is so simple and boring and handled without drama that the *Post* takes absolutely no interest in it no matter how many times Genevieve calls them. Do you get me?"

"I do," I said.

"Can you handle this for me?"

"I can," I said.

I CARRIED THE CAKE HOME on Metro and practiced ways to tell Daniel I was leaving for Wisconsin in a few days. I didn't trust the state: my first job had been in Eau Claire; I had felt dazzled by its beauty and also claustrophobic the whole time, charmed by and hostile toward a region I had never entirely forgiven for its commitment to civility and conflict avoidance. Midwest nice was a steady, polite gaslighting I found sinister, a forced humility that prevented anyone from speaking up when they'd been diminished or disrespected, lest they be labeled an outsider. I was bewildered by the pride the region took in these pathologies. I didn't trust my role at IPH, or at least I didn't trust anymore my assumption that as long as I didn't openly defy the agency, I'd be left alone to do work that mattered. I didn't trust my own motivations. I wanted for once to get something right when Genevieve was wrong, but I also wanted my assignment to the case to be because I was careful and thorough and would ask the right questions, not because my friendly brown face would make good damage control when the agency discredited Genevieve, again. I didn't trust my impulse to call Nick, my last serious ex, who was still in Milwaukee so far as I knew, and tell him I was coming to town, and I didn't trust myself to explain any of it to Daniel.

Daniel and I had met three years earlier, at a happy hour that Elena dragged me to. I'd been restless, nostalgic for the work I'd left: my nearly finished manuscript nagged at me, and it was disorienting having just experienced the second fall in my lifetime that I didn't answer to an academic calendar. I still missed having an ongoing research project, and I had begun to design whimsical minor empirical studies, including one surrounding my wardrobe. When I was teaching, I'd been alert to which classes trusted me most when I was drab, dressed in blacks and grays and covered in a blazer, hair locked into place and makeup subdued, and which trusted me most when I looked eccentric, when my dresses and scarves and jewelry blazed and dangled and my lipstick was always red. There was always a question of how my appearance affected my credibility, but the answer was never the same from semester to semester. When I began at IPH, I tried out different styles on the general public: formal versus informal, eclectic versus reserved, cleavage versus covered. That day's experiment, an elegant blue dress with a moderately interesting neckline and a jaunty scarf, hair pressed flat and then curled again for body, had me looking more than usual the young professional. It fell into the *people were happier to speak with me, but more likely to argue with me about whether I knew what I was talking about* quadrant of my wardrobe chart, and it made me feel out of place at Elena's neighborhood bar, which pulled its crowd from artists and grad students and NGO workers, people who wouldn't recognize me as one of their own in my current ensemble. It was a small thing, but I thought of it often lately: how out of character I'd looked when Daniel and I met, how unlike myself.

I had been sitting in one of a circle of metal chairs outside by the patio heat lamp, which glowed softly and was almost romantic, except that the patio faced Eleventh Street traffic and was sandwiched between a dog park and a rowdy sports bar. I caught Daniel's eye as we were both surveying the landscape.

"Do you know what the problem with DC is?" he said casually, scooting his chair closer as though we were old friends in the middle of a conversation just arriving at a point of intimacy that required us to keep our voices down. It was a habit he had with everyone, something I came to understand as his journalism mode, the one that got people to drop their guards by strolling right past them, but at the time I felt seen, interesting.

"There's only one problem?" I asked.

"Well, no. I mean the reason nobody ever tried to preserve anything until it was too late, the reason we're going to lose all the mom-and-pop operations and corner stores and carryouts?"

"Money?"

"No and yes. The problem is everyone, even Black people, believes that Black poverty is the worst poverty in the world, and Black urban poverty, forget it, and all urban Blackness always scans as poverty, which means people only love us as fetish. No one is sentimental about poor Black people unless they're wise and country and you could put a photograph of them on a porch with a quilt behind them in a museum. There's always a white person out there who wants to overpronounce a foreign word, or try an exotic food, or shop for crafts, but no one wants to do that for Black folks. Once white people started thinking they were better at urban Blackness than Black folks, it was game over. My dad grew up three blocks from here, but his parents lost their town house to property taxes and he can't even bring himself to drive into the city to visit me. Says he's going to get himself arrested one day driving up Fourteenth Street, yelling out the window cursing Barry for selling the city out from under folks."

"Wow," I said. "Are we already at the part where we talk about our families?"

"I don't like small talk," he said. "Tell me about yours."

I did. I was the child of two federal employees, raised in a city where integrated federal jobs had crucially sustained the Black middle class. The most bewildering part of leaving DC the first time was discovering that elsewhere people casually used "federal government" as a pejorative. I needed no convincing of the fatal possibilities of government overreach, of the way the fatalities told the story of who the nation considered expendable, but, even after the low points of the previous decade, I believed in government, or at least believed in it more than the alternative. That my country might always expect me to audition for my life I accepted as fact, but I trusted the public charter of national government more than I trusted average white citizens acting unchecked. I believed in government, I had come to understand, the way that agnostics who hadn't been to service in decades sometimes hedged their bets and brought their babies to be baptized or otherwise welcomed into the religions of their parents' youth. I had abandoned the actual religion I was raised with as soon as I got to college, but when in moments of despair I needed the inspiration of a triumphant martyr figure who made me believe in impossible things, I thought not of saints or saviors but of my mother.

When she was pregnant with me, she'd gone down to Louisiana on behalf of the Justice Department, charged with enforcing a school desegregation order that was nearly older than she was. She was twenty-five and six months pregnant, fresh out of law school and the sole employee sent to investigate. When she arrived, she was shepherded around by eleven different Black people who wanted to make sure that she knew the men in the truck who followed her with shotguns were the local Klan. By the time I was born, the people of that small Louisiana parish had nothing yet but faith and a high school in underfunded disrepair, but they believed in my mother and sent her home with a chest of handmade blankets and bibs and baby clothes, and by the time I was a year old, the parish's Black high school had a science wing with lab equipment and new textbooks. That was the small victory so offensive to the local government that they had been willing to raise weapons in defense of it before the Justice Department in the form of my mother arrived. I asked her to tell me that story over and over, to tell me the name of the person who'd made me each doll or bib or blanket. It was my first experience of faith. It was part of why I'd jumped at the chance to come to IPH—I had imagined it was my best chance to be part of a legacy, something meaningfully bigger than myself.

DANIEL ASKED SO MANY QUESTIONS about my parents and my childhood that I thought he'd forgotten we were flirting, or where the story ended—with me, with my job and my hopes for the future—but after a few minutes he let the conversation wander back.

"So, IPH? When I first saw you, I figured you for something depressing and corporate you were here to drink away your guilt about."

"Is that why you didn't start by asking what I do?"

"I never start there. It's an easy trick for being the least predictable person at a DC party. Ask anything other than 'What do you do?' If people want you to know, they'll still find a way to tell you."

"So are you pleasantly surprised that I'm not a corporate sellout?"

"Do you really think it's a good idea for the government to be in the business of telling people what the truth is?"

"It's not the government, it's me," I said. "And it's not the truth in some abstract ideological sense. It's the actual historical record. I was a professor for three years. I loved teaching, but all my resources went into bringing information to the exact people who would have gotten it somehow anyway. Now I can be anywhere."

"But so can anybody," he said. "What happens when you leave and the office is full of people with a different agenda?"

"I guess I don't leave," I said. "Isn't that the point of being a career civil servant? Administrations come and go and there you are, doing the work. Did you change how you did your job when your newspaper got sold?"

"You strike me as the leaving type," he said, avoiding the question. We both laughed and treated it as though he had paid me a compliment, though later it would occur to me there was no reason it should have been. Things started quickly between us but then didn't seem to know where to go. We were busy; I had recently declared myself to be beyond giddy girlish feelings and their accompanying heartbreak; he'd broken an engagement a month before he met me, though I gathered some months later that while the wedding was off by then, the fiancée hadn't yet entirely disappeared from his life. I didn't pry—there was no arrangement we'd made, and if there had been, the way things were headed I would have held on to it quietly, certain already that someday I'd need forgiveness, or something to hold against him.

TONIGHT I HAD INTENDED a mood for Daniel's birthday: candles, the cake, a change of clothes, my good lipstick. But when Daniel arrived I was thoroughly unmade, the candles unlit, and the cake still in its box. I had shed my pants and bra, but was still wearing a work blouse over yoga pants, sitting on the living room floor with the contents of the clarification file spread in front of me.

"I got you a cake," I called when he walked in. "It's on the table."

"Fancy cake," he said, a moment later. I looked up and found him staring into the cake box.

"I was working Capitol Hill today. I had to go to a gentrification bakery."

"Is there any other kind anymore? I was just talking to a cat who grew up there yesterday. Working on a long piece about what happened to the property people lost to back taxes. Did you at least get to yell at any tourists?"

"Not even one."

"All I wanted for my birthday was a video of you just once cursing out a white person who should know better." He sat beside me and gestured at the papers. "So what did you get me? A scavenger hunt?"

I leaned into him. He had stopped at home, I noted, had changed out of his work-routine suit and into a dress shirt, smelled like good cologne—woodsy and bright—and coconut oil. I kissed him. He began to sort through the contents of the file, and I decided it would be both rude and futile to demand privacy. I gave him the basics and let him look through the records with me.

"I'm sorry I didn't make fancier plans," I said. "I'm trying to figure out what happened to a guy who tried to buy property in the thirties and may or may not have died for it. See? You can hate my job all you want, but we're both trying to solve the mystery of why this country doesn't let Black people keep anything."

"Boo-Boo the fool could solve that mystery. The real question is how we get it back."

"Black love is Black wealth."

"Isn't that poem about being broke?"

"Look, I got you a gentrified cake, a pile of evidence about how much our country hates us, and a Nikki Giovanni metaphor about dealing with it. Happy Birthday. Make it count, because I have to leave town soon to deal with all this—it's a clarification on one of Genevieve's corrections."

"Why don't they just let Genevieve be? It's bad enough they drove her out. Now they can't stop undoing everything she did while she was there?"

"It's not like that. This might be an actual mistake. I have to go to Wisconsin and find out whether or not this man was actually murdered."

"Wisconsin."

"You know that's not it."

"Do I?"

"This is a work thing—I have to make a correction. It might even be a relatively happy one, but I have to do it gently enough that we don't have to go on another apology tour or duel the goddamn Free Americans in the press."

"So you're letting them use you now so you don't have to let them use you later."

"Them who?"

"You tell me."

"I don't have anything to prove," I said. "If there's someplace else you'd rather be on your birthday, I'm not keeping you here."

"I guess you're not," Daniel said, getting up. "But, for the record, this was where I wanted to be."

I refused to meet his eyes. I stared at the floor and waited for the door to slam and then got up and ate two slices of Daniel's birthday cake for dinner. The buttercream was exquisite but the cake itself was dry and crumbly. I overthought the metaphor. I had made the wrong choice,

clearly, but had I made it in trying at all or in not trying
hard enough? The night had probably been salvageable when
I let him leave. Things were always salvageable between
us, and knowing that felt like both a relief and an obliga-
tion. I wanted to be able to go out into the world with him
and protect him from anything that might harm him, and
I knew that I could not; I wanted to leave for Wisconsin
with the freedom to be disappointing and I knew that I
could.

I went back to my documents. The researcher tasked
with assembling clarification files had done a thorough job.
In the file there was an article about the fire from the *Ap-
pleton Gazette* and an obituary that had run later, in the
Wisconsin Enterprise-Blade, calling for an investigation that
of course never came. The *Gazette* article focused on the
chemical cause of the fire and included a photograph of
the damage, but the obituary included a grainy photograph
of Josiah himself, and a bit of biographical detail. Josiah
Wynslow had dimples and an easy smile. In the photo he
looked younger than he had been when he died, but the
stylish hat and suit made me think the picture had been
taken in Chicago and not Mississippi—somewhere there
was still a before Joe, a Mississippi boy who hadn't yet followed the great migration north. So much violence and
lack waiting on the other end of the violence and lack that
people poured out of the South to escape, and still they
kept believing there was someplace in this country where

they could be Black and be safe and make a home. Chicago, at least, had the pull of community in its favor, had decades of sales pitches calling the Black Belt up north, decades of people who had already learned to call the city a home. How was it that Josiah Wynslow had left Chicago and come to believe he could make his home in a place where no one wanted him, had wanted to stay there badly enough to die or cheat death?

.   .   .

Officially, I was staying at a Ramada off the highway somewhere between Cherry Mill and the Milwaukee airport. Unofficially, I had texted Nick from National before my plane took off, and while it was possible his number had changed since we'd last been in touch, or that he was no longer in Milwaukee at all, or that he would choose to ignore my message, I was entirely unsurprised to see him waiting for me at the arrivals gate. His hair was shorter than I was used to it being, and it made his eyes, already a startling blue, stand out conspicuously. We had parted last on bad terms too inconclusive to be permanent. A few years ago he'd come to DC for a conference, and when we'd tried to have a friendly drink, he'd chastised me for leaving my position at GW, accused me of both wasting my talents and working in the service of empire, which seemed contradictory: my job could be menial or it could be gravely problematic, but not both. Now he seemed contrite—he offered a ride and a home-cooked meal. I was committed enough to the premise that we were harmless to each other to insist he drive me first to check into my hotel, and to keep the room keycard in my pocket as though I would need it later, but honest enough that my suitcase didn't make it out of the trunk until we arrived at his loft.

I'd met Nick in graduate school in a different state, and our time in this one had overlapped only by a single summer, at the end of my visiting gig in Eau Claire, and just before he'd started teaching at UW-Milwaukee. I spent most of that summer with him in his half-unpacked apartment, a cookie-cutter basic one bedroom I imagined exactly mirrored the apartment on the other side of the cheap plasterboard walls. When he said he lived in a loft now, I expected he'd stayed in the city and moved into something more aesthetically pleasing, one of those abandoned industrial spaces gone pricey, cavernous, and artisanal, with concrete floors and floor-to-ceiling windows, but, in fact, he lived in what my younger self would have called the woods, though I now knew it was merely rural, and that only barely. Nick's childhood had been odd: he'd grown up monied half the time and rurally pragmatic the rest; his mother was the abandoned first wife of a man who went on to money. He'd gone to boarding school and then come home in the summer to be working middle class; he looked every bit the overgrown prep-school boy, but those summers were the roots he tended to play up. His house was a converted barn, and though I would not have put it past him to have taken his desire to transcend his patrician roots so far that he was now supplementing his academic work with farm labor, he explained that he had bought the barn from the family who used to run the place, and though one of the farmer's children still lived in the house across the field, there was no farming happening anymore, the farm not having the capital to invest in the dairy industry's turn to mechanical labor or the cushion to survive without an investment.

"I did a lot of renovations myself," he said. "But there's no livestock involved, so I hope you didn't come all this way to see me milk a cow."

"I didn't come all this way to see you at all," I said.

When he'd moved here, he'd said it was because teaching at a state school better suited his praxis, though quietly I had heard his leaving had been slightly more contentious than that, that it involved a badly ended affair with a graduate student, which I believed insofar as I had also been a graduate student there, though to the extent that our involvement had ended, it was me who had ended it both times, in each case saved from my own worse impulses by a job in a different state. When we met, Nick was a junior professor and soon to be divorced. We had a two-body problem, he told people, but just going on offhand gossip, by my count there had been at least nine other bodies involved on his part alone by the time his wife called things off.

Such was his level of charm that it was hard to be disgusted by it: Nick expected a door to open and it did; he expected to be adored and he was. Before Nick, I had been eating at the same three restaurants and drinking at the same two bars for years because it spared me the exhaustion of walking into a new place and convincing them I belonged and they should treat me kindly, of greeting clerks and waitpersons in my PhD voice, dropping the name of the university when necessary, generously overtipping. It was a revelation to move through the world with Nick, to see how little attention a white man needed to devote to that kind of performance, how much of his worry about how other people saw him could be consumed by the frivolous, how easy it was for me to be assumed respectable merely by association. It was in some ways the thing I'd liked least about him, even less than things that were actually his fault: when I went places with him, things were easier; when I was with him, the *do they know I'm human yet* question that hummed in me every time I met a new white person quieted a little, not because I could be sure of the answer but because I could be sure in his presence they'd at least pretend.

Though he was a political scientist, not a historian, I had taken a jointly listed class with Nick my first year in graduate school, but our dalliance had not begun until the next fall, when we found ourselves trapped in a cocktail party corner with a drunk senior faculty member who said he wasn't complaining, exactly, about political correctness, but he did miss, sometimes, humor, or the capacity for particular kinds of observation, that he had told a harmless joke and his undergraduates had complained that it was racist. Alarmed that he was going to segue into the joke, and I was about to learn who would laugh and who wouldn't, I intervened brightly to suggest that I too sometimes worried my funniest jokes might offend, for example, *A white man walks into a room.* While everyone waited for the punch line, I excused myself and headed to the porch. *That's it,* I called behind me. *That's the whole joke. Everything else disappears.*

Nick had appeared outside beside me a few minutes later. He put a hand on my shoulder and gave it a firmer squeeze than was comforting.

"I would have said something if he'd told his joke," said Nick.

"Isn't it nice that we'll never have to know if that's true," I said, and after we shared a cigarette we left the party together and stayed intermittently together for the next two years. Once I was alone again, navigating my way through a beautiful but bleak Eau Claire winter and trying to find the people and places welcoming enough to feel like home, I realized I had become so accustomed to Nick's presence that it was surprising again when I went places and people treated me like myself. It was the winter after the most depressing election of my adult life, a low point for my faith in the polis, and I had started keeping an unofficial tally in my head of how much I trusted each new white person I met. It was a pitiful tally, because I had decided most of them would forgive anyone who harmed me, would worry more about vocal antiracism ruining the holiday party season and causing the cheese plates to go to waste than about the lives and sanity of the nonwhite humans in their midst. I couldn't, of course, say any of that aloud, though what minimal decorum I had I'd only recently reacquired: I'd become accustomed to Nick shielding me from the more outrageous things I said. Without him, I had to re-learn a certain modulation. Back in DC, first with men whose birthdays and favorite colors I didn't bother memo-rizing, and then eventually with Daniel, I'd had to learn again how to watch a man move through the world and calibrate his every step to be disarming, how to watch a man worry about his body and the conditions under which someone might take his any gesture the wrong way. I'd had to remember back to high school, when my heart belonged only to boys my color, to whom I had to insist that no one else's disrespect of me was worth a fight, was worth what a fight would cost them. That Daniel could only assume ev-erything about my relationship with Nick had been ex-ploitative bored me. That it wasn't only Nick that Daniel would have hated, but the person I became when I was with him, cockier, more reckless, willing to take it all for granted: that kept me up at night, or at least, sometimes it kept me up, or as a metaphor it kept me up. In Nick's room, in his platform bed, under the locally made quilt, I in fact slept very well.

OVER BREAKFAST we skirted the issue of my purpose for being there. The night before I'd withheld most of the details—pled state secrets and repeated back to him the years-ago insults he'd lobbed at my work. "It wouldn't interest you why I'm here," I said, knowing full well nothing interested Nick like a mystery. At his breakfast table, after eating locally made yogurt and granola I caved and explained the background of the case. I wanted him to come with me and do the magic thing that made strangers in small towns more welcoming, and I wanted, I supposed, another read on the situation.

He offered to drive me all the way to Cherry Mill, since I hadn't picked up my rental car yet. In the car, he gave me what felt like the tourism board's official spiel on everything charming to discover there. I was certain it would indeed be charming, but the Upper Midwest made me moody; people made me feel like I was being asked to speak a language I'd never learned and in which I was constantly misunderstood. When I lived here, it had taken me months to recognize that the pushy advice strangers gave about things like where to buy cheaper bottled water and which store was having a sale were not meant to be intrusive or judgmental or presumptuous but simply friendly, that they were considered friendly whether or not I experienced them that way, and even more months for me to understand that long meandering conversations full of small talk, the kind I considered a brief prelude to real human interaction, were never going to open up into genuine discussions or open expressions of feeling on their own, they were only going to restart on a loop. Once I had offended a Minnesotan colleague at IPH by saying it was no surprise this region was full of serial killers because what could be easier than being a horrifying person in a community where gossip and open conflict were shunned. The next day I found affixed to my desk a corrections sticker noting that most serial killers came from California, followed closely by Florida.

So far as history recorded there had never been a serial killer in Cherry Mill. True cherry-growing country was farther north, in Door County. I'd made the drive up with Nick the summer we'd spent here together and had to concede it was idyllic, even though I didn't like cherries and distrusted lakes. Cherry Mill was in the Fox River Valley, just south of a cannery and situated in between two paper mills. It was close enough to Lake Winnebago that it picked up vacation traffic, though mostly from visitors who couldn't travel far. Still, I recognized in the solicitous festivity of the two blocks that comprised downtown something of the energy of DC in summer, the desperate language of tourist traps everywhere, selling a performance for people eager to believe they'd found whatever they'd come for.

The candy store that we were looking for, the one that stood on the lot that had once been Josiah's, was a redbrick building, but someone had painted a scattering of bricks in bright primary colors, zigzagging down the exterior. The marquee advertised it as THE SUGAR MILL, with a giant lollipop and candy apple, and a handwritten sign in the window suggested the cherry taffy or the brandy fudge, both of which were homemade and on sale. Through the windows I could see the checkered floor and wooden countertops. I distrusted, in general, appeals to nostalgia—I loved the past of archives, but there was no era of the past I had any inclination to visit with my actual human body, being rather fond of it having at least minimal rights and protections. I tried to think of what this block would have looked like when Josiah first set eyes on it, what about it would have called to him.

The sign I had come to see faced the small lot where Nick parked the car. It was unobtrusive, easy not to notice if you weren't looking for it, which had, according to the file, been a source of some contention when the first sign went up in the '90s. The store owner won the placement debate, arguing that she didn't mind having the sign, but no one wanted it to be the first thing children saw when they came to get sweets. Genevieve's new sign was brassier, but still located in the same spot, on the side of the building, near the parking lot:

IN 1937 AFRICAN AMERICAN SHOPKEEPER JOSIAH WYNSLOW WAS KILLED WHEN A MOB INTENDING TO KEEP CHERRY MILL WHITE BURNED DOWN THE ORIGINAL BUILDING WHILE HE WAS INSIDE. THIS TYPE OF VIOLENCE WAS AT ONE POINT FREQUENT ALL OVER THE COUNTRY, AND THOUGH THERE WERE FEW OFFICIAL RESTRICTIVE COVENANTS IN WISCONSIN THEN, IN PART BECAUSE THE AFRICAN AMERICAN POPULATION WAS SO MINIMAL, RACIAL RESTRICTIONS AND THE BOUNDARIES OF "SUNDOWN TOWNS" WERE OFTEN ENFORCED LESS OFFICIALLY THROUGH VIOLENCE OR INTIMIDATION. CITIZENS INVOLVED IN THE BURNING OF THE STORE AND THE MURDER OF JOSIAH WYNSLOW WERE NEVER CHARGED OR PUNISHED IN ANY WAY, THOUGH MANY PUBLICLY BRAGGED ABOUT THEIR RESPONSIBILITY FOR THE CRIME. THE NAMES OF THE INDIVIDUALS KNOWN TO BE INVOLVED ARE GUNNAR WEST, ANDERSON PIEKOWSKI, GENE NORMAN, RONALD BUNCH, ED SCHWARTZE, PETER DETRY, AND GEORGE AND ELLA MAE SCHMIDT. GEORGE SCHMIDT TOOK OVER THE PROPERTY AFTER THE MURDER AND SOLD IT AT A PROFIT IN 1959.

I checked the file. The original sign had started off the same way, but where the identifying names appeared in Genevieve's sign, the original final line had read *Today in Cherry Mill we welcome all as friends and visitors, and are glad to have learned from the past.*

In the front of the shop, a woman was standing in the window flipping the CLOSED sign to OPEN. She was a collage of reds, candy apple lipstick, and hair the color of grenadine, her dress a faded burgundy and her skin freckled and sun-blushed pink. She waved.

"Welcome," she said. "We're open now if you have a sweet tooth."

"It all looks wonderful," I said, "but unfortunately today calls for caffeine before sugar and business before pleasure."

"Business? Are you here with the young lady who came by earlier? The one who kicked up all the fuss a few months back?"

"What lady?" I asked, forcing a smile and arriving at the answer to my own question even before I heard her description of Genevieve.

GENEVIEVE WAS SITTING in the window of the coffee shop, reading the morning paper. She had let her hair grow out a bit since I had seen her last, and now it haloed her face in curls. She was as put together as ever; the heat that threatened to burn everyone else only seemed to make her glow. As though in solidarity with the sun, she wore a bright yellow dress. She put the paper down and raised her eyebrows when she saw me. I told Nick to wander and let me figure out Genevieve on my own. His plan seemed to be merely to walk up and down the block; as I waited for my coffee and then joined Genevieve at her table, I kept catching flashes of him passing the window.

"I heard you were coming," Genevieve said.

"What are you doing here?" I asked.

"I have some free time. My ex has Octavia for the month."

"Why is this what you're doing with your free time?"

"You may recall that I am out of a job of late. But as neither IPH nor academia holds a monopoly on the historical record, I'm not necessarily out of a profession. A little bird at project headquarters told me something interesting might be happening here, so I pitched a feature piece on it."

"You're a journalist now?"

"I'm a storyteller, in any medium. For all I don't love about the West Coast, it's lousy with TV people, one of whom thinks if I can create some buzz there might be a market for me yet. History Exposed with Genevieve Johnson." Genevieve fanned out her hands and framed her camera-ready face. "So here I am. And here you are. Buzz buzz buzz. Have a coffee. It's not bad, for Wisconsin."

"Why would it be bad? They fly the same coffee beans here as everywhere else in the country," I said.

"Wow. Already defensive of the good white people of the Upper Midwest. They're going to feel so much better when you take my mean old sign down."

"I'm not here to take your sign down because it makes people uncomfortable," I said.

"Oh, nice. You decided to finally stand up for something after I was gone. Why are you here then?"

"Genie. This was my job before it was yours and for longer. Just let me do my job. And if you're hitting up people at the office for gossip, next time get the whole story."

"It's still Genevieve. Come on, Cassie. In a different world, if I wanted to know what was happening with one of your cases, I could have called you."

I opened my mouth, impulsively reaching for the first adolescent retort that came to mind—*Whose fault is it that you couldn't call me?*—but before I said the words, I remembered that it was arguably mine.

"I don't need your help," I said. "This might turn out to be a simple fact-check. If it doesn't, you're not going to make it any easier. I'm guessing open-and-shut historical mysteries don't sell a lot of reality-TV pitches. Is that really what you're in this for?"

"As always, I'm in it for the truth. I'm also in it for my custody case, if you need a better reason. James wants primary custody and it's hard to fight that without a reliable income, so, unless I want to be stuck in LA waiting for my alternate weekends and watching him raise my daughter with his pageant-queen fiancée who can't wait to get a tiara on her, I need to come up with something fast."

"You grew up in tiaras. I was there, remember?"

"Cassie, I couldn't possibly speak to what you remember and what you don't."

Genevieve had worn a tiara at her own wedding, I wanted to say, but of course I did not actually remember that, not having been there. I had only seen it in the photographs. When I was feeling uncharitable, I allowed myself to think that Genie and Genevieve weren't so different; both versions of the girl I grew up with wanted most of all to be the center of attention. Then I thought of Octavia, whom I'd last seen as a child who could barely stand to be parted from her mother, whom Genie spoke to and of with a tenderness I'd never heard in her voice in any other context, and I felt cruel for imagining Genevieve would let a mere performance cost her as much as it already had. Whoever she was these days, she believed in it.

The front door opened with a bell chime, and I recognized Andy Detry from his description of himself—he'd said he was a big guy with a big beard and would be wearing a Brewers cap. I'd expected I might find a dozen men fitting that description, but he was the only one in the coffee shop this morning. He introduced himself with a firm handshake. I introduced Genevieve as merely Genevieve, and although she had no idea who Andy was or why he'd come to meet me, she pulled out an official-looking notebook and pen and leaned in as though she too had been waiting for him.

I'd wanted to see Andy in person for a better sense of what I was dealing with—an honest concerned citizen, or a man trying to find the loophole that would get his grandfather off of a list of public shame. Once he started talking, I decided I liked him. He had a nervous laugh, the kind that bubbled up at his own jokes and also when nothing was funny at all, but he seemed genuinely horrified by both versions of what might have happened to Josiah Wynslow.

"I grew up here as a husky gay boy," he said. "Not saying it's the same as knowing what it would have been like to be him back then, or hell, to be me back then, but I know something about how it feels to have a whole gang of people wishing you didn't exist, ya know?"

Most of his story was already in the file: when he saw his grandfather's name on the plaque, he'd decided to do something about it. He ran a bar now and made a decent living and wanted to find out whether Josiah had any next of kin to whom he might deliver an apology or some meager reparations. By all accounts, Josiah had been unmarried and childless when he came to Cherry Mill, but Andy wondered if perhaps there'd been siblings, cousins, anyone. Someone had sent in an obituary, after all. He'd reached out to an amateur genealogist friend and started with vital records, which is where he'd come upon a puzzle: there was a 1937 Wisconsin death certificate for Josiah Wynslow, listing no next of kin, but there was also a 1950 marriage certificate for a girl in Kenosha whose father appeared to be the same man, though it was hard to be completely sure—the 1937 Josiah didn't yet have a Social Security number. He'd gone digging and turned up an Illinois marriage certificate for Josiah and the mother of the woman in Kenosha, and then an Illinois death certificate reporting Josiah had died in Chicago in 1984. His wife had also died years ago, but the daughter who had married in Kenosha still lived there, with one of her daughters and two of her grandchildren. That was how he'd found the relatives I was scheduled to talk to later in the afternoon. They'd told him they knew Josiah had run into trouble in Wisconsin and been run out of the state, but he had certainly run out alive. Andy threw up his hands.

"So, it's a mystery," he said. "I'm not saying they weren't trying to kill him, but it doesn't seem they managed."

I pulled the photograph of the arsonists out of the file.

"What can you tell me about who took credit for it?" I asked. "Anything it might be helpful to know about the people in this picture?"

"Not much I can think of. Everyone in the picture's long dead of course, except the baby, and she's almost ninety. I'd say there's maybe ten people still in town related to someone in the picture somehow. Me. Susan behind the counter there. Susan's mother—she's the baby. Susan's fool nephew. Two of the Piekowski grandkids. And Ronald Bunch's son, but he's on home care and good luck getting past his nurse."

Andy laughed his nervous laugh again. He shifted back in his chair and gripped the edge of the table. I looked over at Susan, round faced and gray haired. She had greeted me with a smile and offered me a muffin on the house because she didn't want me having coffee on an empty stomach, and I'd had to promise her I'd already had breakfast before she let me walk away empty-handed. "They're not bad people, mostly," Andy said. "But they don't talk about it much and probably wouldn't much appreciate me bringing it up again. If anyone knows anything that's not already in the records, they sure haven't told me."

He leaned forward again and started to say more, but seemed to lose the words, instead raising himself from the table and saying his goodbyes. He offered a beer on him if we made it by his tavern. I thanked him and watched him walk out into the sunlight, squinting and shielding his eyes with his palm.

"Not bad people," said Genevieve after he'd left. "What would a white person actually have to do to lose the benefit of the doubt? How many murders would they have to cover up?"

"Six, I think. But we might not even have one here."

"You're talking to Josiah's family next?"

"It's none of your business what I'm doing next. This

isn't your case. It's not even appropriate for you to be here. Take a breath. Have brunch. Let me do my job."

"Do you know how I ended up here in the first place? Originally, I mean. I was in Madison catching up with an old colleague. We went to brunch. Cute little place with sunny windows and red-checked tablecloths and cocktails and mocktails and home-style breakfast foods with ample vegan options. Besides the tablecloths, the decor is all old photographs and postcards that they scrounged up from wherever, because you know how white people love their history right up until it's true. So I'm sitting at my adorable checkered table, minding my business, drinking my basil mimosa, and under the glass I see this photograph. All these smiling faces you see before you. And a burnt building, so that's weird. So I slide the photo out from under the table glass and I see this bit about fire and purification and Cherry Mill and now I'm guessing it's nothing good, and it's such small news, really, just one life out of so many, that I can't even figure it out on my phone at first, I have to go digging in the archives to find the controversy from the '90s, and it's only because someone went digging then that the rest of what I was looking for was even there to be found, and all that's with so much evidence that a whole town knew what happened and a year after it did, the motherfuckers took a group photo and signed their names. That's how easy it is to think you're a person having brunch and realize you're actually a hunting trophy. So, I will wait if you want

me to, but come back when you need me, because like it or
not we are always all we got."

"Do you think I don't know by now how to be careful?"
I asked.

"You know how to be careful and you know how to do
the right thing, but you've never known how to do both,"
Genevieve said.

"Neither have you," I said. "Both may be undoable."

"Strength in numbers," said Genevieve.

I was searching for the way to most emphatically tell
her that this was not an argument, that our discussion had
in fact concluded, when I heard a commotion outside and
looked out the window, where Nick was gesturing franti-
cally. I waved him in. He had gone into a used bookstore at
the end of the block and when he reemerged there was a
commotion at the end of the block. He said we needed to
see it. While he was explaining, Susan at the counter's cell
phone dinged; she propped up a wooden BE RIGHT BACK
sign near the register and walked outside to see what was
happening. We followed her, back toward the candy shop
and the parking lot where we'd left Nick's car. The sun had
picked up and I felt pinned by it even before I saw what
everyone was looking at.

Where not an hour earlier there had been an unmo-
lested sign, there was now an enormous red X covering it
in spray paint, with WE WILL ERASE YOU written and un-
derscored beside it. A smaller, stylized tag beneath the

graffiti read WHITE JUSTICE in jagged capital letters. To the right of the lettering was a nearly person-size rendering of the Free Americans' elk symbol, in the same virulent red. The display covered most of the side of the store.

The woman we'd met at the candy store earlier was at the front of the small crowd, shaking her head and smoking a cigarette. Up close I could see her name tag read KIM. Susan joined her and asked for a light.

"Stupid kid," Susan said, after her first drag.

"You know who did this?" I asked.

"I mean, I didn't see it, I was inside same as you, but I wouldn't need three guesses," said Susan. "Though he's not really a kid anymore—twenty-seven, but for all the sense he's got, he's been sixteen for over a decade now, my mother would say. You heard of Free Americans?"

"Unfortunately."

"Well, there's less for them to do around here than when they first got started up. So they got worked up about the sign when it went up and had a protest outside of the store. Seven of them, marching around in a circle looking stupid. A few years back they had enough of them to look impressive, but like I said, it's died down. I haven't heard much about it since, but outside of them, well, some people didn't like it, but no one else was really angry enough to do this. The guy who calls himself in charge of the group here is my idiot nephew. His real name is Chase."

"Your nephew?"

"Don't hold it against me. I didn't raise him."

"But Ella Mae was his grandmother? Yours too?"

"She was, may she rest in peace. I didn't know about that picture or anything with the store until the first sign went up, which wasn't until after she died, so I don't know what to make of it. To me, she was kind. He was young when she died, and I don't think she has anything to do with whatever Chase is up to. The family reputation has never really been his calling. Kind of killed that the first time he went to juvie. His dad—my uncle—died when he was a kid and hadn't been around too much before that, and his mom—well, she does the best she can. Both of them have a lot of ideas about politics that we don't talk much about to avoid the arguing. We've been thinking for a while he might outgrow it. But doesn't look like he's planning on it."

"It would seem not," I said.

"I better get back to the counter," said Susan, finishing her cigarette and grinding the butt into the asphalt.

"Are you OK?" Nick asked.

"I'm fine," I said reflexively, though I felt shaken. I thought I should call the office and alert them that there might be press after all, but I felt like I'd screwed up already, even though I knew, rationally, that it wasn't my fault. I wanted to blame Genevieve, to imagine that her insistence that this job was controversial and worthy of TV had conjured up the danger and made it newsworthy, but I also knew it wasn't her fault she was right.

"Should we start looking for this guy?" asked Genevieve. "Do you think it's worth talking to the cops?" I assessed her, in her bright yellow sundress and camera-ready makeup. I wanted to laugh, but she seemed dead serious, as though she expected that not only was this now a joint mission, it also included fighting crime.

"I am not going to go chasing a villain who calls himself White Justice. Either a town is going to let a person run around goddamn calling himself White Justice or it isn't," I said. "The police will investigate the graffiti and I will investigate the facts on the sign."

I pressed my fingertips to my temples and closed my eyes. When I opened them again the crowd was thinner, but the graffiti was still in front of me, violent and wet. I felt bad for snapping at Genevieve. Her eyeliner was smudged, like while we had been taking things in, she had been blinking away a tear. I wasn't used to thinking of Genevieve as desperate. I could judge her for courting publicity only because I knew my rent would be paid no matter what happened here, and it wasn't exactly my doing that she couldn't say the same, but I didn't feel good about my role in it. I filled Genevieve in on why I was actually there, and told her I was tracking the past and not the future, so if she wanted to wait for the cops and focus on this part of the story—the present—I'd stay out of her way. I asked if she was going to call the news, hoping I could at least give the director a warning, and when she was sheepish, I realized she wasn't going to call anyone yet—right now there was nothing she had to make herself central to the story, so no reason she'd hand it to a reporter. I retracted my flicker of sympathy.

I walked with Nick to his car, where he put his arms around me and leaned his forehead into mine and asked if I was all right. The intimacy felt startling, a shock and not the fabled spark. I was afraid, and my fear indicted the idyllic morning we'd had, reminded me why I had come here and why I had left him. I had not wanted to be tricked into thinking I was safe—not with men like him, not in towns like this, not in crowds of *good* white people. I pulled away and got into the passenger seat.

"Do you want me to come with you?" Nick asked once he'd settled into the driver's side. "I don't like the idea of this guy being around. He's obviously pretty close, and he may have seen us earlier. That show was probably for your benefit. I can drive and we can get your rental car later."

"What are you going to do if he's following me? Distract him with chitchat about the bylaws of the master race?"

"Do you know anything about whether or not this guy is dangerous?"

"Maybe he's the kind of harmless white supremacist who threatens genocide for fun," I said.

"Cassie," said Nick.

I shushed him in the interest of answering his question

through an internet search. It took a few tries combining keywords, but I summoned the right monster to my phone. White Justice had apparently been posting weekly videos for years. Considering the time he must have put into it, he had a sparse number of followers, but judging from their comments and upvotes they were mostly adoring. The top-rated video was from a year ago, just after Genevieve's sign had gone up. I pushed play. White Justice's large face filled the video window. He had panicked hazel eyes and patchy facial hair and a face that seemed like each individual feature could be attractive, but they somehow didn't work together. His voice was booming, even with the volume low. The video zoomed out; he had given the phone camera to someone else. He stood in front of the sign, in the place where we had just been standing, wearing the trademark ascot and a fedora that appeared to be his own doing. A crowd of about a dozen people in the same getup was gathered near him. He gestured to the sign and ranted at some length, his speech punctuated by cheers. "The point of this is shame!" he continued. "Shame for white people! But we built this city! We built this state! We built this whole country! These people don't build things! These people don't love themselves! If death makes them so sad, where are the memorials to Milwaukee's dead? What about Chicago's? They kill their children! They don't love their children! They hate us and they want us to hate us too! We do not! We are proud! We will fight back! We are the future!"

At that, the crowd joined in—this was one of the Free Americans' rallying cries—*We are the future*—a cheerful way of saying the shame of the U.S. past wasn't genocide or terror but the fact that it hadn't completely worked yet. It was nothing I hadn't heard before, but it was rattling. It was the ubiquity or it was the persistence. It was the way the Free Americans and their claims on being the only Americans transcended facts and time and progress, the way they always seemed to be around the corner, the way, however lacking in general insight they might be, they could somehow hear the ticking clock of the question, the *Do they know I'm human yet?* the way they took delight in saying no, the way they took for granted that it would always be their question to answer.

. . .

The Robinsons, Josiah Wynslow's nearest living descendants, lived in a modest split-level ranch across from a strip mall between Racine and Kenosha. Though the drive was over an hour, I was still an hour early, so I waited in my car in the strip mall parking lot, contemplating the dollar store's window display. I had done my best to downplay that the morning had made me afraid, but now the fear had settled.

The whole drive down I was worried that someone was following me, and that if someone was following me, I wouldn't know what to look for, wouldn't count on help to come if I asked for it. Now that I felt certain I was alone, the tension broke into quiet panic, a general anxiety replacing the specific. The bright yellow dollar sign in the store's window appeared to be floating toward me the longer I stared at it, and I looked back and forth between it and the scrolling red marquee of the check-cashing place next door, as if what I was really looking for would present itself in the juxtaposition, like in one of those 3-D images where you had to find the angle that would reveal a picture that made sense.

I felt unmoored, and so I called the person who made me feel most grounded. When Daniel didn't pick up, I texted him to say that I was here safely and sorry I'd ruined his birthday and that I was a little shaken up because the local white supremacist fuckboys apparently knew I was in town. I sent him a picture of the graffiti. My phone didn't ding. I pushed down the seat and lay in the car, waiting to cry but feeling mostly depleted.

At two, I composed myself and left the car to ring the bell at Ms. Adelaide Robinson-formerly-Wynslow's house. A teenage boy answered the door. He had wide bright eyes and a soft smile. He was wearing a wave cap and a jersey and a brand of jeans and sneakers I hadn't seen in the wild since the late nineties. I had the disorienting sense I had around teenagers lately, that because they looked like they had walked out of the malls of my childhood, they were speaking to me from the past. He introduced himself as Anthony and led me to the living room, where I felt my breath calm. It looked like a living room I had been in before. The furniture was floral and leather, all of it covered in knit slipcovers; the walls were studded with every child in the family's school pictures, on one side an old family portrait, and on the other side, framed portraits of this household's trifecta of Black saviors, Jesus, MLK, and Barack Obama. On the table there was a tin of butter cookies, open to show it still had cookies in it and had not yet been turned into a sewing kit. A box fan sat in an open window and they had left me the seat directly in its path. Anthony introduced me to his mother, June, and his grandmother Ms. Adelaide. His father lived there too, but was still at work, driving a city bus. June was Ms. Adelaide's youngest, in her forties, and already in salmon-pink scrubs for her shift as an orderly that started in a few hours. Her hair was tucked back, but her face was radiant, her eye makeup impeccable, and her lipstick a darker shade of pink that picked up on the color of the scrubs and, like a photo filter, turned them from sickly to elegant. Ms. Adelaide was nearly eighty, I knew from her birthdate, but she was sprightly, quite dressed up for a weekday afternoon, which I briefly flattered myself by thinking might be on my account. I worried that she'd gone through too much trouble for me, until she confessed she was hoping Anthony would run her to the casino after we were done, a request it seemed his initial refusal would do little to impede. June offered me a glass of iced tea and went to the kitchen to get it for me even though I told her she didn't need to. I made small talk until June returned with the glass, cold but already gathering condensation. She sat in one of the wooden chairs and scooted it forward until she was almost between me and her mother, not hostile, but protective.

"Grandpa Joe's been dead going on twenty years now," June said. "So if the law's looking for him you can tell them they're too slow."

I laughed. "I'm not here about anything he did wrong. I am here about when he died."

"I know I don't look it," said Ms. Adelaide. "But I was born in 1947 and my daddy was a Josiah Wynslow who got run out of Wisconsin before he was my daddy, so he certainly couldn't have died there, could he now? So, now that we got that covered, is someone finally about to do something about that crazy white boy before he kills somebody?"

"What boy?" I asked.

"First I even heard about any sign or any Cherry Mill was a fool sending me evil letters. Called me everything but a child of God and said he would not let us defile his family name. I hadn't the slightest what he was on about until Anthony talked to that other man. Meantime, June took one of the letters to the police, but, you know police. Lord knows what his mama calls him, but the boy calls himself White Justice."

"I believe his mama calls him Chase," I said. "I haven't met him and hope not to, but we think he spray-painted the memorial sign this morning. How long has he been bothering you?"

June explained that he'd been sending them threatening letters for months. I asked to see them, and she sent Anthony to fetch them, and the family records while he was at it. I looked at the letters first, wanting to get the ugly part out of the way. They were vile, but written in perfect penmanship. It frightened me how neat they were—the kind of letters that for all their crazy had clearly been drafted first, the kind of neat readable letters a person wrote if he expected there to be a reason for them to be public someday. It seemed characteristic of the present that everyone, even the worst of us, was practicing being famous. I had no jurisdiction, and no reason to believe the local police would care if the director of the institute called them, but I photographed them anyway, for Genevieve if for no one else, and told June and Ms. Adelaide I wasn't sure if it would help any but I would have my boss follow up.

After the letters, the family archive box was a relief. I had already seen Josiah's Illinois death certificate, but Ms. Adelaide showed me the archaic family Bible, which she, as his oldest living child, was now the keeper of. His birth and death had been recorded along with everyone else's. He had been the second child of four—an older brother who died young, a younger brother who had lived to be ninety, and a sister who had no recorded year of death. I asked if I could see a photograph of Josiah; Anthony brought me one from the wall, June brought me an album, and Ms. Adelaide rummaged through the box until she found the one she was looking for. In the photo from the wall, Josiah was an older man, but he had the same face he did in the photo I had seen in the file.

In the album, June pointed out for me a dozen pictures of him, and I watched him come back from the death he'd been assigned in 1937 and marry, grin lovestruck at his wife, wear the uniform of the plant he'd worked at, hold his babies on his lap, cut up dancing at their weddings and graduations, grow old. It was the photo Adelaide had pulled from the box, though, that made me certain I could close the file. The picture had been taken at the Chicago Savoy, late in the 1920s judging by the fashion and the posters in the background. Josiah had his arm around a cream-colored woman with roller-set hair, and they both wore grins and roller skates, both looked delighted and post-dance breathless. I'd seen that smile—literally, I'd seen the same smile in the photograph in his obituary, the same light suit and dark shirt and patterned tie, the same hat jauntily askew on his head. Our file had been missing the woman, and all the evidence of the decades he had yet to come, but I had the same man.

"We'll get this cleared up for you," I said after I'd scanned the photo with my phone. "Probably what will happen is the sign will come down, and hopefully that will keep that man from bothering you anymore anyway, if the police don't follow up."

"Don't hold your breath on them," said June.

"Can't they just fix the sign to say they burned his place down and he escaped?" asked Anthony. "They still stole."

"They did," I said. "But our sign was just a correction of the original sign. We've had a hard time with cities even wanting to memorialize the dead. I don't see much chance of getting anyplace to make a note of every piece of land or property that was stolen. And we can only correct what's already there to be fixed. I'm sorry."

"At least he made it out of there for us to be here," said June.

"Can I ask if you know what he was doing here in the first place? In Wisconsin?" I asked. "Not a lot of Black people or work for Black people here in the middle of the Depression. Why did he leave Chicago?"

Ms. Adelaide took a sip of her tea and sat back in her chair. Instinctively, I leaned forward to hear her.

"Of course, I wasn't around back then. And he didn't talk about it much. But Ma'dear did sometimes. She had four children. Three boys, including Daddy, and Minerva in the middle, but Minerva was always treated like the baby girl. That's her in the picture with Daddy. He came out to Wisconsin looking for her."

Although my official assignment was finished, clean enough that I thought my answers would satisfy even Genevieve, I couldn't help myself. Curiosity was an occupational hazard. I asked how it was Minerva had come to need finding. According to Ms. Adelaide, Minerva had been born restless, which, in her defense, being born a Black woman in Mississippi in 1910 might make a person. The whole family—Josiah, Minerva, their parents, and their two brothers—had left rural sharecropping and gone to Jackson after the first wave of great migrators made room for them to find work in the city. It was supposed to be the oldest brother, Elijah, who first left Mississippi for Chicago to test the waters and get a job that would send home train fare for the rest of the family to come up, but when he'd almost saved the money to go, Minerva, who was sixteen then, stole it from the coffee can under the floorboards and added her own paltry savings. It was enough to get her out of town. "Too big for her britches and too big for a small town," Ms. Adelaide put it. Minerva had been reading *The Defender* and was certain that in Chicago, fame and fortune awaited her and she could send for everyone else sooner than Elijah would. By the time she realized the Chicago that greeted her was already overrun with buxom light-skinned country girls who had pretty faces and decent voices and thought they could model or sing, and no one had been waiting for her in particular, she was already there and didn't have train fare home.

After nearly a year as a boardinghouse maid, where Minerva found herself terrible at cleaning and in constant need of the lady of the house's interventions to keep boarders from making passes at her, she got her bearings. With the recommendation of the landlady, who found her cleaning subpar, but appreciated what she could do with flowers and decor, Minerva got a job as the apprentice florist at a Black-owned shop that got most of its work from being partnered with one of the neighborhood's Black funeral homes. She was pretty and charming enough to upsell grieving families, and passing contact with the dead and grieving didn't make her squeamish, so she was good at the work. The family who owned the shop treated her well, kept her busy, and paid her a decent wage.

Elijah broke his leg the next farming season and never did leave Mississippi, where he married and started a family, so it was Josiah who came up a few years later. When he came to Chicago in 1928, it was Minerva who taught him to navigate the city. It was her beside him in the photograph I had seen, the little sister who, even grown, brought out the laughter in him. The photo must have been from the last of the good years, because by the '30s there was no more Savoy money, no more Brownie camera or anything that could be sold for cash, and no work for Joe—he had a city name now, but no city job anymore. Minerva rode it out OK for a while, because even if funerals and flower arrangements got smaller, people didn't die any less often because they were poorer, and the death industry seemed Depression-proof. But she didn't have enough for two people to live on, and Joe followed the promise of work from recruiter to recruiter, and city to city for a few years, during which he blamed his not hearing from Minerva on his lack of a permanent address. By the time he resettled in Chicago, three years later, the florist had gone under and Minerva was gone, and no one could say where.

"She just disappeared?" I asked.

"For a while she did," said Ms. Adelaide. "Some people said she'd gone back to cleaning houses, and some people said they'd seen her making time with some white man, but he wasn't around either by the time Daddy got back to town. When my grandparents finally came up to Chicago, they had a letter she sent home to Mississippi, saying she was doing all right. It was years old at that point, but it was the last anyone had heard from her, so when Daddy saw the postmark was from Wisconsin, he at least had an idea of where to go after her."

"Did he find her?"

"Not the way he told it, but I don't think Ma'dear ever believed that. Minerva never came back anyway. Back then I suppose a white man could have done anything with a

Black girl once he got tired of her. But the way Ma'dear talked about Minerva, seemed she'd have just as likely killed that man as let him put a hand on her. Always had her eyes on something bigger. You know the type. Couldn't stand the thought of just being a regular Black girl and having to do like everybody else. Ma'dear always figured my daddy found her and she told him she didn't want to be found, that she would rather be disgraced or come to a bad end than come back home."

I looked more closely at the woman in the photograph. In the picture she was barely more than a teenager. Her mouth was open in a laugh, but her eyes were steel. It was unclear who was wobbly on their skates, but in the picture she and Joe were hanging on to one another like they were each the only thing keeping the other person upright.

"You see?" said Ms. Adelaide. "You can see the trouble in her. Like I said. You know the type."

* * *

I left the Robinsons with an anticlimactic sense that my job was both done and forever undoable, a simple matter of reconciling the record books and an impossible matter of making any kind of actual repair. I had three messages from Genevieve, one telling me that she'd heard more Cherry Mill gossip than she cared to but knew nothing about the current whereabouts of White Justice, another telling me she was safely in her B & B for the night and I could find her there if I wanted to tell her what I'd found, and a final message in which she essentially repeated the second message, but with a desperation that sounded disorientingly unlike her. "Come on, Cassie," she said. "Call if you find something out. I need this." I had one message from Nick, who had reservations at a tiny place where he was on a first-name basis with the owner, asking if I'd meet him there for dinner, and one message from Daniel, who I called back right away. He was concerned, and we picked up the conversation as though we were not fighting. I summarized my trip so far, being honest enough to say that Nick had come with me to Cherry Mill, but not volunteering where I'd slept. I told him about Genevieve, and the graffiti, and the Robinsons, and my nagging question: Who had taken the time to write to Wisconsin's struggling Black paper and report that Josiah was dead, and beloved, when his family knew he was very much alive?

"Maybe he wrote it himself?" I thought out loud. "To prove his own death and buy himself time to start over? To leave a record of what happened?"

"The man was running out of town and stopped long enough to write his own obituary? And call himself 'beloved'? He doesn't sound like a man with more ego than sense."

"Give me a better idea then," I said.

"What about the sister?"

"What about her? No one knows where she was."

"Doesn't mean she didn't know where he was."

"So what happened to her?"

"Cassie. What happens to Black people when they don't want to be Black anymore?"

The answer felt obvious now. If you wanted to hide Blackness from white people, you went where they would least suspect it. At the turn of the twentieth century, a Black Milwaukee lawyer claimed offhand that hundreds of the white people in Milwaukee were actually Black people passing. There was nine-to-five passing for employment, and there was sometimes passing, and then there was the kind you disappeared into, the kind you might not come back from. *You know the type*, I thought. *You know the type.* A second answer to the question nagged at me. I felt confident Daniel was right and queasy about the possibility that I might also be. I got off the phone before I could say it out loud and make it real. I told Daniel I had to call Genevieve, but instead I took a nap and a shower. I dressed with the intention of having dinner alone at the hotel bar, but when I got to the lobby I felt daunted by my own suspicions, and annoyed by the dinging of my phone, and so I muted it and kept walking to the parking lot, where I got into my car and drove to meet Nick, as I supposed he'd known I would.

Outside, the restaurant was an inconspicuous old farmhouse with a chalkboard sign, but inside it had been redone, rustic, and chicly minimalist. The tables were unfinished wood and the chairs were modernist and metal. The ceiling beams were exposed and the wood flooring was salvaged, but the art on the wall was blocky and bright. Schubert piped in from invisible speakers and the menu was the genre of farm-to-table where the waiter introduced meat and produce by county of origin. I sulked through two glasses of good wine before we were done with appetizers.

"Smile," said Nick. "You're at the best hidden gem in Wisconsin."

"I'm pretty sure the best hidden gem in Wisconsin has cheese curds and three-dollar spotted cow."

"I've known you too long for you to pretend this place is too fancy for you. You're not a dive bar girl."

"You haven't really known me for years."

"I wouldn't have to know you for five minutes to know that. I'll take you for a dive bar beer later if that's what you want. I've been worried about you all day. I don't like the idea of some half-cocked white supremacist tracking what you're doing."

"I don't love it either, but I don't do this work to be chased off by the first two-bit white supremacist with a paint can."

"It's Wisconsin. If he isn't armed with more than a paint can he could be in five minutes. Do you know he's the head of a rogue branch, officially? I've been reading about him all day. He's been formally expelled from a quasi-libertarian organization best known for starting street fights. Not a guy you want to get into it with."

"I'm going to recommend the sign come down anyway," I said. "Not for the reasons he wants, but it will solve the problem. All evidence would suggest that Josiah Wynslow died an old man with a loving family in 1984, and all the good people of Cherry Mill did was use his imploded build-ing to steal the land they were never going to let him keep."

"Then why don't you look happier? Case closed. Mostly no one gets a second act in America, so here's to Joe, who got the hell out of hostile territory alive and met a nice girl and had some babies and died of old age. May we all be so lucky."

"He had a sister. He followed her to Wisconsin. That's what he was doing here. She never turned up, not even after he supposedly died. I think maybe that's who sent in an obituary."

I pulled out my phone and showed Nick the image of Minerva I'd scanned earlier. I zoomed in on her face.

"Do you think you'd know she was Black? If you hadn't seen that many Black people?"

"It's hard to tell in black-and-white. You think she was passing?"

"Maybe. It would explain why she cared enough to write an obituary but never got back in touch with her family to find out if he was still alive."

"So then say she was passing. Then he lived and so did she. They both cheated the rules and beat the system."

"The house always wins."

"You don't believe that."

"Don't I?"

You know the type, I thought. *You know the type.*

. . .

Following Nick's car back to his place, I tried to convince myself I saw things his way: two people made themselves a way out where there wasn't one, there was nothing left for me to do but set the record as right as it could be. A way out of what, though? In the driveway of the lofted barn, I looked at the red paneling and the big windows and the bright hanging moon. I pulled Nick through his front doorway and led him up his loft stairs and into his own bedroom, trying to be a woman without baggage, a woman who did not believe the worst was always coming. I deliberately did not check my phone. Let it be as happy an ending as it can be, I told myself. I decided to change my flight and go home a day early. I wasn't responsible for knowing the unknowable and I wasn't responsible for what Genevieve did next and I felt deliriously not responsible for anything as I pulled Nick into his bedroom and whispered what I wanted, undressed him button to button, button to zipper, ignored the nagging voice. Later, awake in the cool sheets and in the clarity after my second orgasm, I felt suddenly, queasily sure of what was true, of the connection I'd been avoiding making for hours. I pushed the thought away long enough to sleep for an hour, but woke again as if startled out of a nightmare. I looked at Nick's sleeping face, but instead of calming me, it reminded me how easy it was to slip into wanting something, how easy to become something else by wanting. *You know the type.*

I got out of bed and fished my phone out of my purse. The screen awakened to reveal a cavalcade of updates from Genevieve: everyone in Cherry Mill knew Chase had done the graffiti but no one knew where to find him or how to prove it. I had one message from Daniel, a zoomed-in photo of the photo from the file, one he must have snapped before I'd left DC, before our fight. He knew I'd see it, probably that I had seen it already and spent hours trying not to know the words for it. I opened my phone and looked again at Minerva's face in the photo of her with her brother. I scrolled back to the magnified face of Ella Mae Schmidt. I looked between them until I was certain that looking back at me from Ella Mae Schmidt's haughty expression was the face of Minerva Wynslow. There had been something ugly to me about Ella Mae's presence all along, something about the set of her eyes against the florals of her dress, the baby on her hip, the feminine softness and lipsticked grin beside the triumphant aftermath of violence. I had imagined into Ella Mae's expression a particularly vicious innocence, the innocence of white women who never saw the damage in their wake, and now I tried again to understand what I was looking at. Ella Mae could have pretended innocence, but Minerva would have known better.

I showered in the guest bathroom so I wouldn't wake Nick and, though it was barely dawn, called Genevieve from my rental car in the driveway. I had intended not to need her, but I did now—it was a revelation I didn't want to be alone with, one I understood I didn't want to walk away from, although there was nothing forcing me to follow up on it. It will be good for Genevieve's story, I told myself. Let Genevieve have it. As though I was gifting her something, and not running from it. The phone went to voice mail the first time, but she answered my second call groggy and alarmed, and agreed to meet me at a twenty-four-hour diner off the highway outside of Cherry Mill. I drove there entertaining a choose-your-own-adventure of self-loathing: at some point Minerva Wynslow had become Ella Mae Schmidt, had gone from a girl who fled the Mississippi summer for the promise of a city life, a girl who laughed with her brother's arm around her, a girl who wanted more but cared enough to write home, to a woman who smiled outside the building where her brother had died, who boasted of having set it aflame, and then, her brother presumed dead, stayed Ella Mae long enough to have a child, who had two children of her own, one of whom had a son, and now the great-grandson Ella Mae never met was generations removed from his own Blackness, was vandalizing Josiah's memorial, terrorizing his distant cousins, and proclaiming a violent willingness to defend the integrity of the white race.

I arrived before Genevieve and waited for her in a plastic booth. It was the hour of the day when the diner was mostly empty except for truckers, who ate silently and alone. I drank my coffee and hoped for the clarity of Genevieve telling me my eyes were bad and my deductive skills were bullshit, but when she arrived and slid into the booth across from me, and I showed her the two pictures side by side, Genevieve caught on faster than I had.

"Are you fucking kidding me?" she said. "White Justice isn't white?"

"You want to try telling him that?"

"Sure. Let's find him and slap on a correction sticker citing the one drop rule. Problem solved."

"The Office of Historical Corrections finds that you are in fact Blacker than the Ace of Spades."

"The Office of Historical Corrections regrets to inform you that you are so Black you got marked absent in night school."

"The Office of Historical Corrections has concluded that you are so Black your credit score dropped one hundred points as soon as the bank saw you in person."

"The Office of Historical Corrections wants you to know

that you are so Black the apartment you went to see was coincidentally just rented right before you got there."

"I like it when we're friends," said Genevieve.

"You could have fooled me," I said.

"You called me," said Genevieve.

I FOLLOWED GENEVIEVE'S CAR back to Cherry Mill. We had decided to start with Susan, our only direct line to Ella Mae, but didn't have a plan beyond that. It was only because there was no plan that there was a "we." We both parked in the same downtown lot as the day before, and I looked in the direction of the sign and the graffiti, but it had all been covered with a white tarp that was affixed to the side of the building, I supposed until it could be power-washed or muraled over. It covered everything: White Justice's artwork, but also the original sign. The coffee shop was just opening for the day, only Susan and two customers inside, and the homey haphazard upholstered chairs and twee memorabilia marking the walls made me feel more on edge. Susan greeted us warmly, but her face pursed when I asked if it would be possible for us to speak to her mother.

"If this is about my nephew, I promise you we haven't heard from him," said Susan.

"It's not about the graffiti," I said. "We'd like to talk to her about your grandmother."

"My mother gets tired easy," Susan said. She was reluctant to say anything further, but when we said politely that we'd just look up the address and go ourselves instead of troubling her, she agreed to bring us over if we could wait an hour for the shop's other employee to show up. I ordered muffins because I felt irrationally guilty about being in the shop without buying anything, and too jumpy for a second cup of coffee. For an hour, Genevieve and I sat together in the cozy chairs and waited.

"And you thought I didn't have a story," she said.

"We don't even know what the story is," I said.

I was not looking forward to the rest of the day, but Genevieve, I could see, was excited about it. It was one of the differences between us that had been true even when she was Genie—she liked talking to people more than I did. She had the nerves for the uncomfortable conversations I only forced myself to have in the interest of the larger purpose. In grad school, though I wasn't proud of it, I'd sometimes mocked Genie's areas of focus, joked to our peers that she'd gotten as far from studying Blackness as she could. I was jealous, of course, partly that by avoiding the academic race beat, Genie had sidestepped the daily trauma of the historical record, the sometimes brutality and sometimes banality of anti-Blackness, the loop of history that was always a noose if you looked at it long enough. But I was also jealous because Genie's primary sources were long dead, discoverable only through paper trails. Mine I often had to track down and ask to speak to me about the worst days of their lives, a task I categorically knew that Genie would have been better at.

SUSAN DROVE US a few miles to her childhood home, which was sturdy and wood framed and had been in the family for generations. Abigail still lived there, as her parents had before her and her father's parents had before that. Owen Varner, Abigail's husband, had died a decade earlier, but the inside furniture tended toward plaid and the decor toward hunting trophies, and though the animals he'd mounted must have been dead for more years than he had, their glassy-eyed awe made them seem still afraid. In the living room, there was a portrait of a younger Abigail and Owen, and Abigail looked enough like her mother that I had to look twice to be sure the portrait was of her and not her parents. The sunporch where Susan led us was lighter than the living room, its furniture fraying wicker. Susan offered lemonade, and while we waited for her to bring it I looked up, the peeling paint on the porch roof showing glimmers of blue and green beneath its current coat of white, and tried to remember whether painting your porch haint blue was a Black tradition or just a southern one. Susan returned with a pitcher of lemonade and then left and came back again with her mother on her arm.

Abigail Varner was eighty-eight years old, and though she walked slowly and seemed to need Susan to steady her, her voice was sharp and clear when she greeted us, and her face could have passed for two decades younger.

"Like I was saying yesterday," Susan said, "I'm sorry about my nephew, but we can't tell you why he's causing trouble. The downtown association had an emergency meeting yesterday and we'll get the mess cleaned up. But my grandmother doesn't know where Chase is any more than I do."

"He hasn't called in months," said Mrs. Varner.

"We came," I said gently, "to ask a question about you. About your mother, actually, if that's all right."

Mrs. Varner straightened up.

"You'll find my mother's not here to answer for herself. When they put her name on that sign I didn't fuss, or pretend that wasn't her in the picture, but if you came to ask me to speak ill of the dead, you've come to the wrong place."

"I put her name on the sign," said Genevieve.

"Well then I guess you know what you think of her. I can't imagine what you came here to ask me."

"How much do you know about your mother before she came to Cherry Mill?" I asked.

"As much as anyone knows about their mother before she was a mother, I suppose. The stories I was told. She had a beautiful laugh and sang like a bird, but she wasn't a big talker. She was in Chicago and working the counter of a flower shop when she met my father. It was love at first sight. My father walked in for a bouquet for the poor girl he was dating at the time and walked out with a wife. She came here with him and never looked back, and they were in love until they died a month apart, and they probably still are in the hereafter if it allows that sort of thing."

"That's a lovely story," I said.

"Isn't it?" said Mrs. Varner.

"It sounds a little bit like the story I heard about this woman," I said, sliding the picture of Minerva to Susan and Mrs. Varner. "She worked at a flower shop too, but on the south side. When it closed, she disappeared, and eventually wound up in Wisconsin, where no one ever heard from her again. But say she didn't vanish into thin air. Say your mother wasn't originally from Chicago, but from Mississippi, say she came up on the train, in the colored car, where they would have made her stay because beige reads differently in Mississippi, and on the south side, than it does in a place where there wasn't enough mixing to know what mixed looks like. Say when that south side flower shop closed up, she took herself to a neighborhood where the florists could survive the decade, one where they didn't know what she was, and when she left that neighborhood she left with a man who brought her right here. Then say her big brother followed her. He did some work, not all of it legal, and came into some money, and bought a store for cheap, on account of it was the Depression and the land he

wanted was way outside of Milwaukee and dirt cheap because the owner was trying to keep afloat. Maybe the owner
thought it would all be a laugh because that Black man
could give his last penny to have his name on the deed and
they'd still never let him keep it, and maybe her brother
should have known that, but wanted to think he could
keep an eye on his sister without blowing her cover. Instead the building ends up burning down while the whole
town thinks he's inside of it, and while no one seemed to
care about anything but getting the property, which, coincidentally, your father did, there was someone who loved
the man enough to send an obituary notice down to the
paper, to mourn him or to cover for him so the white men
wouldn't keep looking. It would make sense if that person
was his sister, except a year later, with the place still a heap
of rubble, there was his same sister in a photograph, laughing about having helped set the fire."

Mrs. Varner tilted back in what I realized was a rocking chair, her face impassive, and kept rocking for just long
enough that I wondered if she was going to pretend she
hadn't heard me, if, in fact, she'd been following at all. A
tendril of her hair had flattened to her forehead in the
heat, even with the shade of the porch.

"That's certainly a story," she said finally.

"Is this not your mother in the picture then?" I asked,
pointing again to Minerva.

"There's a resemblance. But it's not a very good photo."

"She never told you anything other than that she was from Chicago?"

"What my mother told me and what I need to tell you are not the same question. If that was my mother, she would have given up everything she had to have this life and give it to me. If that was my mother, the only reason she would have ever told me anything about any of it would have been as a warning."

"We believe this is your mother," Genevieve said.

"I don't believe you can prove it. And if you could, if that man was her brother and he didn't burn up with the building, someone must have woken him up in the middle of the night and told him to go. Someone must have cared that much, at least. If everyone thought he was dead, was she supposed to up and die too?"

"Is that what she told you, or what you told yourself?"

"Does it make a difference?"

"Did you ever tell your grandson about any of this?"

"What would it matter? The thing about one drop of blood? It's only you people who believe in it now."

. . .

The first time I was ever in a bar, I was with Genie. We were in high school, and not friends, exactly, but we knew the rules that applied to most of our classmates didn't apply to us. By high school we had reached a kind of détente during school hours—I was writing mediocre poems and serving as class vice president, and Genie was on dance team and Model UN and captain of debate club. We each stayed out of the other's territory. We both had boyfriends at high schools that were not ours, and when we went to what we thought of as real parties, the ones where nearly everyone was Black, we went with the boyfriends and didn't consult each other, but when we went to school parties, we went as a pair. We blamed arriving at parties or clubs or shows together on our parents' insistence that we keep an eye on each other in situations that could go badly, but in reality, both sets of parents believed their own daughter to be the sensible one; it was the two of us who our buddy system made feel safer.

Although she was by most measures more popular, I enjoyed myself more than Genie did when we went out with our classmates. Genie navigated social occasions as she did everything else—strategically, and with an eye toward what social currency they could bring her and what a misstep would cost. I liked the opportunity to surprise people with the less guarded version of myself, liked the rush of getting away with things.

Genie had to tell me when I was about to press my luck too far, when I was too much with the wrong person or in the wrong place. Only once had I needed to be the moderating force. Our junior year of high school, a classmate invited us to watch the mediocre band he played bass in open for a better band, and a group of us went to a club to watch. In the middle of the set I realized I'd lost track of Genie. I found her, in the sticky-floored back barroom, doing a fourth shot of tequila—the first two rounds had been earlier, at the band's insistence, but the last two she'd done alone. She was drunk enough that it wasn't worth asking why, so I got us in a cab and held her hair while she threw up on my lawn, and called her parents to say we were having a sleepover, which we were insofar as she passed out inside. In the morning I brought her ibuprofen and water and oatmeal before my parents were awake, giving her a chance to be presentable when she greeted them, which she did with perfect poise.

Alone again, I asked what was wrong. She told me she'd lost a debate tournament, or rather not lost but come in second, and also not lost because she had, by all accounts and measures won, been fiercer and smarter and more polished than the girl who beat her, won by every metric but the judge's scorecards. Her teammates had sympathetically shrugged it off as one of those inexplicable decisions, and her parents had given her the twice as good for half the credit lecture, when she wanted, just once, for someone to tell her that she was already good enough and it wasn't all right if the world wasn't fair enough to reward it, wanted someone to acknowledge that even this trivial thing was allowed to hurt, and that the particularity of the unfairness had a name.

"Genie," I said. "Fuck those people. You're smarter than all of them."

"I am," said Genie. "But it's never going to be enough."

THAT, I RECOGNIZED as I watched Genevieve nurse a second morning beer at Andy Detry's bar, was what had upset me seeing her yesterday. It had reminded me of the only other time, in any incarnation, I'd seen her look defeated. When we'd come in, Andy had been happy to see us and asked how things were going. I told him only the happy version of events—the truth of Josiah Wynslow's long and full life. He gave us the promised first round on him, and he was pleased to hear how Josiah's life had turned out. If he wondered why we were drinking so early to good news, bless the state of Wisconsin, he didn't ask. When we had tucked ourselves into a back booth, Genevieve demanded to know why I hadn't told him the rest of the story, and I said officially I had no rest of the story to tell—no proof of Ella Mae's real identity and no official purpose for proving it.

"So now what?" she asked.

"Now nothing," I said. "I go back to DC and send a request to vital records to pull the incorrect death certificate, and I recommend the city take the sign down, which I assume they will gladly do. I came to answer the question of whether the man survived. I can't do much with a theory about how."

"So what's your theory? Minerva saved his life and kept the property because that's what he would have wanted, or Minerva was a cold-blooded bitch who would have let her brother die to keep her new life and he ran when he saw it?"

"I don't know. I'd like to think the former. Either way, the cost of raising her daughter the way she wanted is that she's got a Black white supremacist grandson running around, so in the end we all lose."

"The beauty of motherhood is that all the choices are wrong," said Genevieve.

"Is it terrifying?" I asked. "Being a parent?"

"Yes," said Genevieve. "It's like every day since Octavia was born I've had to choose between trying to do the best I can for her and trying to do the best I can for the world she has to live in. I wouldn't forgive her for it, but I understand the choice Minerva made in a way I wouldn't without Octavia. She's perfect. She's doing a summer music camp and she's lead violin. How much would I give up to protect her from everyone who's going to hate her just for being there? Look at this. Look at how damn amazing she is."

Genevieve scrolled through the pictures on her phone for me—Octavia onstage, Octavia in pajamas in a picture she'd covered with sleepy emojis by way of texting her mother good night, Octavia making silly faces, Octavia helpfully screenshotting and circling in red ink an advertisement for the Disney princess salon, suggesting they go when Genevieve got her back next month, Octavia giving her own voice-over guide to a makeup artist's tutorial on the screen behind her, giving Genevieve advice for how to do her lipstick when she got famous. I hadn't seen Octavia in real life for a few years, and now, nearly ten, she looked startlingly like Genevieve when I had met her, except she appeared on the verge of laughter in every single picture, and even as a girl, Genie had been serious. In the middle of the slideshow, a new call popped up on-screen, and Genevieve excused herself to take it outside. I nursed my beer and thought about asking for another. When Genevieve came back, she looked tense.

"You OK?" I asked.

"My agent. I don't have enough. He thinks we can't pitch this story on an interesting theory. Not enough open conflict."

"What, he wants you to DNA-test White Justice in the town square?"

"He'd love that, probably." Genevieve took a breath. "Do you think it would change anything? If we told him the truth?"

"I'm sure it wouldn't. People can convince themselves of anything if they want badly enough to believe it."

"Why are you doing any of this then? If you don't think telling people the truth makes a difference?"

"I'm not sure," I said, and I had the strange experience of hearing myself say something I knew to be true only once I'd heard it come out of my own mouth.

"Now you don't care about the job?" said Genevieve. "You damn near acted like I was invisible for a year. You, the person I used to be able to at least count on not to have the sense to stay out of trouble. You didn't stand up for me because you didn't want to."

"I didn't think it would be better if neither of us was in the office."

"Ella Mae didn't think it would be better if both she and her brother had to be Black."

"That's not fair," I said, though I couldn't shake how personally I'd taken *you know the type*.

"It's not fair," Genevieve conceded. "You wouldn't watch me die. But you get away with so much. It doesn't bother me as much as it used to."

"Thanks. I love you too, Genie," I said.

"It's going to be Genevieve forever. But I look at my daughter and I think sometimes that's what I want for her. A life where she doesn't feel like she has to answer to anyone."

"Did you just call me a role model?"

"I would deny it in court."

"White Justice would deny his Blackness in court but that doesn't make it true."

"Yes, well. At least I have a story to break."

"There's no more story here. The story's dead."

"It's a story if I talk to him."

"He doesn't seem like a great talker."

"I need this to work. I can't go back to LA with nothing."

"Genie, you're brilliant. You don't need to rile up an idiot in order to validate your career."

"Don't play stupid. Of course I do."

GENEVIEVE AND I STAYED at the bar long enough to have a third round, and then a round of coffee, which we nursed until I felt sober enough to drive her back to her car. It looked like rain, one of those flash storms that would pass through and leave the day sunny, not strong enough to signal the tornado sirens, but nasty enough that we'd want to be inside before it came. The wind had picked up and the white tarp over the sign billowed. I told Genevieve to go home and sleep, to call her daughter, to find another story, and she said she could promise me only the first two.

I took my own advice and went back to my hotel room to nap. I hovered at half awake, my dreams upsetting and not subconscious enough to be actual dreams. I gave in and decided to go toward the fear instead. While it stormed outside, I opened my laptop and watched an hour of Free Americans videos, trying to make myself immune to them. It felt unfair, how absurd someone could be and still be terrifying. I watched video after video of white boy and "white" boy, cherub-faced and angular, blond and brunette, sharply styled and scruffy, all mangling their country's history in its purported defense, promising to fight for the return of an America that, as they described it, was as real as Narnia. When I couldn't take it anymore, I went back to bed and finally fell asleep for real, but I woke up after only an hour, with the Free Americans' rallying cry of *We are the future* circling in my head. I tried Genevieve on the phone, thinking of Octavia, of the fact that maybe Genevieve was the closest thing I had to a sister, because what was a sibling but a person you stayed tied to whether or not you liked them. She could not stay here, I decided. I had given her this story and I had to take it back, even if I had to put her on a plane myself.

It had stopped raining and was barely dusk now. Genevieve didn't answer. I decided to go in person and talk her out of whatever nonsense idea I was sure she was planning. Five minutes from Genevieve's B & B, my phone beeped to life, and after a minute the messages became so persistent that I pulled over to find out what was wrong. I assumed at first, with the flood of Genevieves on my screen, that the messages were all from Genevieve telling me to turn around and not sabotage her moment, but instead it was a tumble of messages about Genevieve, messages from Nick, and Elena, and Daniel. Daniel's message told me to go somewhere safe and not to watch the livestream; Nick's message had a link, which I clicked.

White Justice's grainy live feed appeared. He was filming on his phone and the angle shook and shifted. First his whole face took up the screen, enraged, and then the camera went to Genevieve's. She had taken down the tarp and was standing where the sign and the graffiti were, where I had seen her just a few hours earlier. "This bitch," White Justice said, "thinks she can come to my town and lie about my family," and as the camera rocked I could see that he was holding the camera in one hand but in the other was a gun. Genevieve had settled her face into a terrifyingly calm expression, although she was armed only with an IPH printer—I wondered if she'd kept hers when they fired her but realized belatedly that it was mine, that she must have taken it, impatient with me, with the lack of purpose with which I was using it. In the background of the livestream I could hear what sounded like sirens on their way, and I willed Genevieve to just keep quiet, to stall until the police got there, although I knew that this would not happen and that even if it did it might not help. Genevieve pointed to the wall, to the silver scroll she must have placed there, her correction of the correction. She read it to the camera, her voice fighting with White Justice's, breaking only on Ella Mae.

"IN 1937 AFRICAN AMERICAN SHOPKEEPER JOSIAH WYNSLOW WAS BELIEVED TO HAVE BEEN KILLED WHEN A MOB INTENDING TO KEEP CHERRY MILL WHITE BURNED DOWN THE ORIGINAL BUILDING WHILE HE WAS INSIDE. IN FACT, HE ESCAPED WITH HIS LIFE, THOUGH THE CIRCUMSTANCES OF HIS ESCAPE REMAIN UNCLEAR. CITIZENS INVOLVED IN THE BURNING OF THE STORE AND THE MURDER OF JOSIAH WYNSLOW WERE NEVER CHARGED OR PUNISHED IN ANY WAY, THOUGH MANY PUBLICLY BRAGGED ABOUT THEIR RESPONSIBILITY FOR THE CRIME. GEORGE SCHMIDT TOOK OVER THE PROPERTY AFTER THE MURDER AND SOLD IT AT A PROFIT IN 1959. ELLA MAE SCHMIDT IS BELIEVED TO HAVE BEEN JOSIAH WYNSLOW'S BIOLOGICAL SISTER, PASSING AS WHITE FOR SO LONG THAT HER OWN CHILDREN AND GRANDCHILDREN NEVER KNEW THE TRUTH OF HER CONNECTION TO JOSIAH OR THEIR OWN ANCESTRY."

"Say it again," said White Justice, cocking the gun.

"You heard me," said Genevieve.

"I'm not a nigger," said White Justice.

"Neither am I," said Genevieve.

I closed my eyes. I didn't know what I was waiting for to know that I could open them, and then I heard the clear crack of the gunshot. Rain, I wanted to think. Thunder. But I knew what I'd heard, and I kept my eyes closed. I pictured Genevieve, not now, but years ago, the last time I remembered seeing her through my own tears, the first time I remembered hearing a sound I thought was a gunshot. It hadn't been a real one. Our high school was doing active shooter drills and an administrator had sprung for the too-authentic training module, and I had missed class the day they'd warned everyone to prepare. When the noise came over the loudspeakers I hid in a hall closet instead of going to the nearest assigned safe room and stayed there panicked for more than an hour, even after the next class bell rang and the hallways were full of clearly alive people and it started to dawn on me that it had only been the facsimile of the violence I'd been waiting for. I stayed in the closet until a teacher noticed I was missing, and Genie offered to look for me and walked the hall calling my name. Even once I left the closet, I couldn't get it together to go to class, and so Genie had walked me to the girls' room and let me cry it out, and when I finally finished she asked, "Are you done now?"

"I didn't know it was fake at first," I said. "You always think when something like that happens you're going to be the bravest version of yourself. I thought I was ready, and I wouldn't be terrified."

"Oh, Cassie," Genie said. "No, you didn't."

Acknowledgments

It would take another book to properly express gratitude for everyone who has made me feel like a part of their community, lucky to be a writer, lucky to be a reader in this moment, and able to write these stories.

Thank you to my agent, Ayesha Pande, a friend and advocate whose faith in my work kept me working. Thank you to my editor, Sarah McGrath, whose patience let this be the book it needed to be, and to Sarah, Alison Fairbrother, and Delia Taylor for being smart and careful readers whose feedback and conversation elevated the writing and made the work of revision a pleasure. Thank you to everyone at Riverhead for taking such good care of my first book, being so supportive of this one, and not yelling at me when I said I was writing stories and a novella.

Thank you to Yaddo, Ragdale, and the Ucross Foundation for residency space; thank you to PEN America, the National Book Foundation, the Hurston/Wright Foundation, the Paterson Fiction Prize, the Nellie McKay Fellowship at UW–Madison, and the National Endowment for the Arts for their support of my career; thank you to the Literature Department at American University, the Creative Writing Program at UW–Madison, and The Writing Seminars at Johns Hopkins University for providing community and writing time. Thank you to the colleagues in all three places whose work provided inspiration and whose kindness made three different cities feel like home.

Most of these stories were initially published in literary magazines. Thank you to *American Short Fiction*, *Barrelhouse*, *Callaloo*, *Columbia: A Journal of Literature and Art*, *Medium*, and *The Sewanee Review* for giving them homes, and thank you to the editors who solicited or selected them and whose early input made the stories stronger: Zinzi Clemmons, Nate Brown, Adeena Reitberger, Roxane Gay, Adam Ross, and Tom McAllister. Thank you to Heidi Pitlor, Meg Wolitzer, and Roxane Gay for honoring two of these stories with inclusion in *Best American Short Stories*. Thank you to Susannah Tahk and Liz Wycoff for reading the earliest versions of several of the stories, to Liz again for fielding some Wisconsin records questions for the novella, and to my colleague Jean McGarry for her feedback on a later pass of the book.

For being my community during the years I needed it most, thank you to Liz, Susannah, Brigitte Fielder, Jonathan

Senchyne, Jennine Crucet, Rachel Louise Snyder, Sugi Ganeshananthan, Brandon Dorman, Erin Gamble, Lily Wong, Melinda Moustakis, Nate and Thea Brown, Adeena Reitberger, Sara Ortiz, Nandini Pandey, Alice Mandell, Charles Huff, Alexis Pauline Gumbs, Elena Diamond, Patrice Hutton, Shangrila Willy, Jeanne Elone, Miriam Aguila, Afua Bruce, Jordan Zweck, Colin Gillis, and Tia Blassingame. Thank you to my family, especially Georgette Dawn Bedoe Brown and, as ever, my father, Walter Evans, for their love and support.

This book is, among many other things, about grief and loss, and about women unwilling to diminish their desires to live full and complex lives. It is indebted to many people who have openly shared their griefs and their joys with me, but was also shaped by my own losses during the years I was writing it. I am thankful for my memories of my aunts Carolyn Evans (1949–2016) and Susie Fillyow (1956–2017), without whom there is less warmth and laughter in the world. Thank you to Beth Ausbrooks (1930–2017), whose life was an example in deciding what was possible instead of letting the world decide it for her.

My love and gratitude forever to my mother, Dawn Valore Martin (1957–2017), whose determination made me believe in the possibility of a better world, whose love made me believe in myself, whose love for telling stories made me believe in their power, and for whom I will be trying to find the right words for the rest of my life.